# *Imagining Argentina*

## LAWRENCE THORNTON

Doubleday   New York   1987

Lines from "The Man with the Blue Guitar" reprinted from *The Collected Poems of Wallace Stevens*, by permission of Alfred A. Knopf, Inc., copyright 1936 by Wallace Stevens and renewed 1964 by Holly Stevens.

Library of Congress Cataloging-in-Publication Data

Thornton, Lawrence, 1937–
    Imagining Argentina.

    I. Title.
PS3570.H6678I4  1987    813'.54    87–5376
ISBN 0-385-24027-9

for Toni

*In any war there are people who disappear.*
—GENERAL LEOPOLDO GALTIERI,
JULY 1982

The man bent over his guitar,
A shearsman of sorts. The day was green.

They said, "You have a blue guitar,
You do not play things as they are."

The man replied, "Things as they are
Are changed upon the blue guitar."

And they said then, "But play, you must,
A tune beyond us, yet ourselves,

A tune upon the blue guitar
Of things exactly as they are."

—WALLACE STEVENS

IMAGINING ARGENTINA

# 1.

Even now, six years after the generals loosened their hold on Argentina, after their manicured hands were pried away from the delicate white throats of the disappeareds and the doors of certain buildings were closed and locked, even now Carlos Rueda's gift retains its mystery. If, in Buenos Aires, the supernatural were woven into the daily lives of people, as it is in the Amazon where natives believe numinous spirits invade the birds and beasts, his accomplishments would be easier to discuss. But we have long been hostile to the things of the spirit, less amenable to them than the rocky stretches of Tierra del Fuego are to a sense of security. Our city is like a sophisticated dowager whose soul feeds on cynicism, a place where the mere mention of the unknown and unknowable occasions peals of bitter laughter. And yet it was here that night after night Carlos Rueda entered the darkness where our people disappeared, spinning words round ghosts and specters until sometimes the people only he could see stepped forth from his imagination into the astonished arms of loved ones. It is all as quick and close as memory, and I want to open memory now, part the curtains upon the fearful, hopeful faces of those who came to the garden of Carlos' house in Calle Cordova because they had nowhere else to go.

Imagine a warm night, a garden filled with the scents of cyclamen and roses and Carlos speaking earnestly to silent people who have drawn their chairs close, or sit on the grass, or on the flagstones of the patio. Among them are Rubén and Clara Mendoza, who have lived for six months at the far edge of anxiety. During that time no word about Pepe, Marianna, or Angela had appeared in the papers, no mention of son, daughter-in-law, or grandchild had come from the lips of those lucky enough to be released. For six months the Mendozas lived as if afflicted by a wasting illness. At home they tried to avoid looking at the photographs and mementos scattered around their apartment, objects as dangerous as broken glass, which they could not bear to put away because their presence seemed to offer a faint hope. Although they developed the habit of tunnel vision, and went from room to room with the exaggerated deliberation of the blind, there were always unguarded moments when they suddenly confronted the smiling face of the vanished son, or daughter-in-law, or grandchild. It was the same when they went out. No matter how careful they were they inevitably turned into a street and saw a tree Pepe climbed as a boy, or the shop where they took Marianna the day she told them she was pregnant. Then memory tore the scabs off their wounds, exposing the thin and sickly nature of their hope. And so one night, out of desperation, and with their sorrow stretched taut as the skin of a drum, they took a bus and came to Calle Cordova.

For an hour they listened to people describing what they knew about their loved ones' disappearances, and then they listened to Carlos tell stories about these people, saying things there seemed no way for him to know. Finally Rubén summoned the courage to speak, and afterward Carlos looked up at the lanterns hanging in the trees and began talking about Pepe, and Marianna, and Angela. It was a terrible story, but it also contained something miraculous. I see the Mendozas exchanging glances, holding each other, and the way hope dimmed into distrust because reason insisted, even to such desperate people, that Carlos Rueda was nothing but a charlatan. Yet on the bus later, the life in the streets, the gleam of neon signs, passed unseen as they followed Carlos' injunction to go home and wait.

Toward midnight there was a faint knock at the door. Rubén left the chain on so that it opened only a few inches, just wide enough to see a young man and the shoulder of someone else. His voice was so soft that Rubén barely heard him when he said, "We have something for you. Please open the door." As if in a dream Rubén raised his hand in slow motion to the chain, his mind filled with agony and wonder at the repetition of the words Carlos had spoken only hours earlier.

"It's all right," the young man said. "Don't be afraid."

The chain rattled against the frame, and as soon as Rubén opened the door the man who had remained out of sight stepped forward and placed a rolled-up blanket in Rubén's arms. Without another word the two men went quickly down the hall, and the elevator doors had closed on them before Rubén and Clara parted the folds of the blanket. Clara shrieked, crossed herself, and went down on her knees. Rubén's hands began shaking and he gave Angela to his wife and then ran for the bathroom. He was confounded by joy and anguish as the sickness rose in his throat. Had St. Jude empowered Carlos Rueda to restore the child, or was the man who had foreseen this a shaman who belonged in a smoky hut deep in the jungle? Rubén knew only that the men had come and Angela was there. He heard her crying as he vomited into the basin.

All this I know because I was there that night in Carlos' garden, and I was there the next day when the Mendozas returned to thank him and Rubén stammered that he had been taken ill because in Angela's face, in her incredibly white skin and bright black eyes, he saw the living tombstone of his son and daughter-in-law, read inscriptions which had yet to be chiseled into polished granite: Pepe Darío Mendoza, b. 1950, d. 1977; Marianna Elena Mendoza, b. 1953, d. 1977. And even though Rubén said nothing about it, he may well have seen a green Ford Falcon disappearing into the night streets of Buenos Aires, its exhaust a stain of gray blood on the air.

And so, with the memory of that green car before me, of the deaths of Pepe and Marianna, of Angela restored to her grandparents, it is time to take a stand about Carlos Rueda, about his stories and their impossible powers. Something beyond our understanding took place which I must bear witness to, something so remarkable that I wonder even now what it means to our conception of reality, for the indisputable fact is that in the darkness of our Latin Night and Fog Carlos Rueda found babies, men, women, even whole families. Is it any wonder, then, that I call his gift a mystery?

# 2.

At the time Argentina was destroying herself I had retired from full-time journalism, though I hadn't stopped writing. Although I lacked the courage to openly confront the regime, I did my part by producing vitriolic sketches I published under a pseudonym in a French magazine. I thought I might collect them later under the title of *The Argentina Notebooks of Martín Benn*, but now, in the face of Carlos' imaginative triumph, they look pitifully inconsequential. Instead I have decided to tell Carlos' story while I am able, before it is distorted by opportunists from all over who have started hanging around his house, the Children's Theater where he works, even around the Café Raphael, which serves as my informal office.

For reasons which will become clear shortly, Carlos confided in me from the very first. Because of what he said, and what I myself have witnessed, I have been forced to think about the way "reality" is parsed and construed, intersected by logic and the laws of probability. I was a man who respected facts enough to make them his profession, and there I was, suddenly facing a version of reality where those hitherto sacred facts, and the empirical method I relied on to discover them, crumbled into dust. Had anyone told me ten years ago that one day I would seriously entertain, without benefit of alcohol, the possibility of a metaphysics, I'd have laughed in his face. Well, I'm not laughing, and I want to tell why I changed my mind, but to even begin to understand you must know a little about Argentina, and about Carlos and his wife, Cecilia.

Cecilia came to work on *La Opinión* in 1970, six years before I retired. One day she was taking final examinations at the university, the next she walked into a newsroom filled with crusty chauvinists hoping she'd fall on her face. Such attitudes did not dampen their libidinous fantasies—her figure was as good as the best on the beaches of Buenos Aires or Rio, and her dark hair, her lovely blue eyes, and easy smile left them gasping for breath. I prided myself for immediately recognizing her ability as a writer and took her under my wing, so to speak. We became friends and soon she, Carlos, and I formed a bond.

Cecilia is even more hard-minded than I am, whereas Carlos' intellectual life is wholly metaphorical. That may explain why he is the chief playwright of the Argentine National Children's Theater. When I first met him at an Italian café in La Boca he seemed shy and withdrawn. It was hard to understand what a woman like Cecilia saw in such a passive man, but as soon as he began talking about his work, I knew. In that little trattoria smelling of cheap Chianti and pizza he talked about his plays and ideas for others that were just emerging, and even then I glimpsed his ability to think beyond boundaries, which, of course, led to things that ought not to have happened. His whole body became animated and his language took off, reminding me of those novelty lamps whose clear plastic rods carry light from the base to the tips where it explodes like a shower of stars.

I liked him immediately, but I must admit that I was also drawn to him because of his resemblance to my son, Tomas, whom Elizabeth and I lost shortly after his tenth birthday. Carlos was just a little older than Tomas would have been if he hadn't drowned in the Plata River while playing with some friends. Since Tomas was just a child when it happened it was virtually impossible to interpolate a mature personality, but I did the night I met Carlos. It comforted me to think that Tomas might have been like him.

After Tomas died in 1956 Elizabeth and I tried to believe we weren't drifting apart for the next four agonizing years. Then one day, in a sudden burst of tears, she said I looked too much like Tomas and always reminded her of death. That was the end, and after our divorce I couldn't look at myself for months. Work sustained me, and when I wasn't working, there was booze. I continued damaging my liver after my editor assigned me to Saigon where my pessimism matured between 1965 and 1969 in the stench of smoke and burst bodies.

By the time I left Asia my mind was filled with indelible images: explosions in the night, which always looked like fireworks from the rooftop of the Caravelle Hotel; the poor; the multilated; the whores so numb they never stopped smiling. Back in Argentina I found that I could look at awful things and remain unmoved even after writing about them, when emotions have a habit of creeping in. I knew I was in trouble, and it was then that Cecilia and Carlos dove into that murky water and brought me up to a different world, restoring me by simply being who they were. I became a member of a family again, and it was not long before their daughter, Teresa, started calling me Uncle Martín.

The next six years were among the happiest of my life, and even now it seems impossible that they ended so abruptly. Almost overnight scattered violence erupted into riots and then troops were swarming in the streets. Everything speeded up, the way it does in old films, when martial law was declared, and I was frightened because history got itself hopelessly mixed up. The Americans and Vietnamese, concentration camps and gulags, Afrikaners and Argentines seemed to utter the same obscenities, the spittle from one gaping mouth burning into people everywhere. I was simply imaginatively unprepared to accept our generals' need to squeeze all opposition out of the country, to purify, to wring themselves dry in an orgasmic rush of violence they hoped would leave them sated and lying beside a prostrate Argentina they had fucked to death: the soldier's dream.

That dream is embedded as a bronze marker in the paving stones of the Plaza del Congreso. All distances in our country are measured from Kilómetro Cero which shines, bronze in sunlight, in the cold eyes of the generals and in the medals cascading over their tunics. In 1976 the generals drew a line around Kilómetro Cero. "Step over it and we will kill you," they said. "The last thing you want to do is to step over this line." They even invented a name for what they were doing, the *proceso*, the process, but those of us watching and suffering had another name, *la guerra sucia*, the dirty war. Even now it seems bizarre that the war was largely carried on with clumsy Ford Falcons whose purpose was to transport the regime's enemies to jails, detention camps, or fields. License plates obscured, they cruised the city's streets like something out of Bosch, moving as deliberately as green beetles I have seen on hot summer nights in Mexico.

Argentines reacted to these preying things more or less like the citizens outside Belsen did to the horrors behind the fences, except that we found refuge in a phrase, rather than silence. *"Debe ser por algo,"* we said, "It must be for something." And then we shrugged our shoulders, said things were beyond our control, that it was better the communists were suppressed because at least there wasn't anarchy. Only a handful of people spoke out. Yes, in Argentina, the spiritual home of *machismo*, the only substantial resistance came from women, especially a group who marched in the Plaza de Mayo wearing white kerchiefs to symbolize their rage and sorrow as they carried signs demanding the return of their loved ones.

Even before the mothers appeared to goad our conscience Cecilia was waving her editorials in the generals' faces. The last one she wrote dealt with some high school students in La Plata who had been agitating for cut-rate bus fares. The generals perceived their grievances as "subversion of the schools," and within a week a bus was found abandoned on a country road. All that remained of the fifteen students who had been on board were three textbooks and a girl's sweater. Cecilia focused on that sweater, how it was handmade for a girl who wasn't even fully grown. She asked how much lower the generals were prepared to sink and demanded the immediate release of the children. Reading it reminded me of a stone sculpture. I could feel the rough texture, see the chisel marks, and I knew it wouldn't be ignored.

It wasn't. It was read in the highest places, as well as in sidewalk cafés, parks, living rooms, at kitchen tables. The afternoon it came out Cecilia disappeared, and I like to think that when it happened her words were heavy on the air, that, as the security men approached, her words were sounding in the minds of thousands of Argentines, and that those who ordered her abduction were frustrated in their knowledge that they could not also abduct her words, smash what she had said.

That thought was in my mind the next day as Carlos and I tried to console each other. We were out in the garden, and he'd begun to tell me what he'd pieced together about her disappearance when he suddenly broke off and gestured toward the patio where family and friends had gathered.

"That's what has become of Argentina," he said bitterly. "A house full of tears."

# 3.

At five fifteen P.M. on May 23, 1976, Pedro Augustín had been repairing the trellis by the front door of his house. As he stooped to pick up the wire he'd brought from the workshop Cecilia turned off Avenida Arboles onto Calle Cordova. She pulled up in front of his house and rolled down the window on the passenger side. Pedro Augustín remembered that she seemed happy reminding him of dinner on Saturday.

A few minutes later, Emilia Lagoda happened to look out her kitchen window just as her neighbor parked her red Peugeot across the street. The window was open, and she heard Cecilia singing a popular song as she unlatched the gate and went into the court-yard. She wanted to tell Cecilia that she and her husband would be late on Saturday because his cousin from Rio was in town, but her children were hungry, and she turned away from the window to finish preparing their dinner.

At approximately five thirty-five Alfonso Márquez, who delivered groceries from Beltran's market to the residents on Calle Cordova, parked in front of Pedro Augustín's house. On the way back to his van after taking the sacks in he saw Cecilia leaving her house with three men. When they reached the sidewalk she turned and tried to go back, but the men pushed her toward the green Falcon, whose left rear door was opened from the inside. Alfonso slid down behind the steering wheel as one of the men got in the back seat with Cecilia. As the car drove off she turned and looked back, and Alfonso said she appeared to be shouting.

Carlos returned from the Children's Theater at six, tired after the day's work. He wanted to talk to Cecilia about the new play he'd been working on and was surprised that she did not answer when he called as he let himself in. Kafka, the cat, who normally greeted him with metallic purrs and a flurry of rubbing against his leg stayed under the dining room table. When Carlos saw the plate of *crudités* on the table he thought Cecilia must have run short of something for dinner and had gone next door to the Pasquales, or across the street to Emilia's. On the sideboard next to the table a copy of *La Opinión* lay open to her story, "La Plata's Children." He had not seen the final draft and thought he would read it before she came back, so he poured some sherry, put on a recording of Villa-Lobos, and stretched out on the sofa in the living room.

Cecilia had not returned when the stereo shut itself off. Carlos checked his watch: it was now six-thirty. As the phone rang Kafka shot out from under the table. Emilia wanted to talk to Cecilia about the dinner on Saturday. When Carlos told her Cecilia wasn't home Emilia said she had seen her come in about an hour and a half earlier. Carlos said he would have Cecilia call when she returned.

Carlos took Kafka into the kitchen where he put a plate of dry food on the floor before dialing the Pasquales. He let it ring fifteen times before hanging up. It was silly to be alarmed, he thought, looking out the sliding glass doors opening onto the garden. There was no sign of her, but he went out anyway, following the brick walk around to the front courtyard in case she'd gone out to gather herbs. The jade plants looked strange, and the plantains seemed to float above the empty lawn.

By the time he returned to the back of the house his heart was beating rapidly. Uncertain about where to look next, he closed the glass door and entered their bedroom where her glasses lay on the floor. At the same time the front door opened and he heard Teresa's voice. When she came into the bedroom and saw him she put her things down and took two steps toward him.

"What's wrong, Papa?"

He put his arms around her.

"What's the matter? Where's Mother?"

"I'm not sure."

"What?"

"Teresa, I think they've taken her."

As soon as he regained control of himself he called the police and then got hold of me. I offered to come right over, but he said there was nothing I could do and asked me to wait until the next day.

I didn't sleep more than two hours that night. Until then the obscenity of what was happening had been at a distance, like the explosions I used to see from the roof of the Caravelle Hotel. Now it was close up and I could see the flash, the yellow searing, feel the heat. When I arrived the next morning Carlos looked haggard from sitting up with Teresa all night, and Teresa was red-eyed and tearful. The police had still not appeared.

As soon as I went inside Carlos pointed to the plate of wilted *crudités* and said that he knew something was wrong the minute he saw it the night before. Then he said he wanted to canvas the neighborhood and Teresa insisted on going along. He asked me to wait for the cops, who finally arrived a few minutes before he and Teresa returned.

I didn't like them, I've never liked cops, and there was no question that the two who showed up were there merely for appearance' sake. We didn't talk. After I let them in and explained that Carlos wasn't back I sat down with a book. One of them thumbed through the day-old paper with Cecilia's story, while the other went out to the car and talked on the shortwave.

When Carlos and Teresa came back they told the cops they'd talked to everyone on the block. Only Emilia Lagoda and Pedro Augustín had seen Cecilia. (They found out about Alfonso Márquez a few days later.) Carlos seemed to be comforted when they wrote down what he said in their little black notebooks and promised to file a report with the proper authorities. As they got into the car the tall one laughed, though when he turned and saw me standing on the porch he tried to look grim, the bastard.

Friends and family descended on the house soon afterward. I couldn't tell whether Carlos was relieved or uncomfortable. I think he wanted to be alone, and accepted them for Teresa's sake. When one of the aunts picked up the *crudités* Carlos looked distressed. He clearly attached something final to those dried-out vegetables and could not bear to have them taken away. When he touched the woman's hand she seemed to understand and they remained on the table throughout the day, slowly losing their color.

It was then that he took me by the arm and guided me out to the garden, leaving Teresa with one of her aunts.

"It's like dreaming about being in a strange country, Martín. You don't know how you got there, and when you speak to a passerby he answers in a language you don't understand. I couldn't believe what I said to Teresa last night. It felt like someone else talking inside me."

And then the guilt started to pour out. I suppose it was inevitable—a clumsy, unconscious attempt to make up for imagined inattentiveness. In any case, he blamed himself. He said he had felt uneasy as soon as Cecilia began writing about the disappeared, but he knew she couldn't look the other way, even if he asked her to. Her confidence helped him accept the danger. Only a few nights earlier someone phoned and warned her to stop writing. She dismissed it as no more dangerous than a pervert randomly dialing until a woman answered. He'd wanted to believe her and tried to put the worry out of his mind.

He'd been looking out into the garden as he spoke but then he turned back to me and his eyes were so sorrowful that I had to force myself not to look away. He wanted assurance that it wasn't his fault, that he hadn't been negligent, and I gave him what I could, though it obviously wasn't enough. How could it be? Most of the time nothing remarkable happens to people close to you. Their familiar eyes are translucent, allowing you inside. But with tragedy it's different. The irises grow darker, become more expressive, the feeling so concentrated that you wonder if it isn't the eyes, after all, which are the true seat of understanding. You try to enter because you care about the person, but the eyes tell you there is something you cannot know and then the sense of entrapment comes over you, the awareness that we are enclosed in a set of feelings impossible to share. That was what Carlos' eyes were like in the garden. He was cut off by his grief and there was nothing I could do but listen.

"I shouldn't have believed her, Martín. I should have made her stop."

That comment seems even more stupid in retrospect than it did at the time. What could he have done? Locked her in her bedroom? Forbade her to act like a journalist? It was completely out of character, part of the fantasy spawned by his guilt. I suppose his fuzzy thinking was the result of shock, of a mind which hadn't time to catch up with his emotions.

I stayed with him until five that afternoon when the pain of Cecilia's disappearance and the fatigue from talking to people I didn't know got to be too much. I told Carlos that I'd call first thing the next morning and then took a cab to the Café Raphael where I drank more than I should have. I'd heard enough about kidnappings to know that nothing could be done, and I was persuaded that if they hadn't already killed her, she was as good as dead.

# 4.

For the next few months Carlos grieved the particular grief of ignorance, his dreams casting up horrifying scenarios from which he woke exhausted and confused. His work suffered, and while he was ashamed of his inattention, he could not stop imagining the scene in his house, especially the way Alfonso Márquez said Cecilia had looked out of the back window of the Falcon.

Later he said that that period was like an intermission in a play whose meaning he could not grasp. It's painful to remember because we saw things so differently. Cecilia's disappearance seemed final to me, and that made it almost impossible for us to talk, especially since Carlos was obsessed by every move Cecilia's kidnappers were likely to have made. He had pinned down Emilia as to what she had seen, crossed-checked times with Pedro and Alfonso. I listened patiently, wondering when the day would come when he would accept that she was gone for good. I tried to bring it up, gently, sometimes, but he always headed me off with one speculation or another.

I'm convinced things would have continued like that indefinitely if Carlos' principal actor, a thirteen-year-old named Enrico Garcia, hadn't failed to turn up for rehearsal one day. Carlos

27

needed him for an important scene they were preparing, and repeatedly called Enrico's house, always getting a busy signal. When he finally got through the mother burst into tears as she recognized his voice. "They took my husband last night," she said.

After he'd hung up he stayed in the office for so long that Silvio Ayala, the production manager, finally came looking for him. Then Carlos went out front, but his heart wasn't in the work. He felt terrible, and the action on stage seemed filtered through a grid of green Falcons.

Finally he gave it up and came to see me. I wasn't much help, I'm afraid, and that was because I really didn't understand his feelings. There was no reason to think it was anything other than normal sympathy for the boy. I tried to draw him out, suggested a film, but he left soon after he arrived, saying that he needed to spend some time with Teresa.

Enrico did not turn up for a week. On the following Monday he appeared backstage looking thin and ill, with dark circles under his eyes, as if he had the flu. Carlos said how sorry he was and encouraged Enrico not to lose hope. Sometimes they only kept people a few days for questioning.

"Not Father. He spoke against them at the university. He said it was terrible what happened to the reporters."

After rehearsal Enrico did not go to the soccer match with the other boys. Still in costume (I think he played a gaucho), he sat with his feet dangling over the edge of the stage, staring into the darkened theater. Carlos suddenly felt very close to Enrico, as if he'd entered the boy's mind, and it was then, with no warning, no intimation of any kind, that the story began to unfold in his imagination. He saw the father, Raimundo Garcia, lying on a narrow bunk with his eyes closed. Someone screamed far off down a corridor and then Raimundo Garcia's eyes opened and Carlos saw pure terror as Raimundo listened to the footsteps approaching his cell.

For a moment Carlos felt insane, then he thought he was hallucinating. Remember, this was the first time it happened, and the experience must have been similar to what one feels under the influence of a powerful drug. As he stood there looking at Enrico the images of the father continued to evolve as in a film, except that it was all there, complete, without the retarding factor of time.

His first instinct was to dismiss the images as aberrations, but as he saw how miserable Enrico was he remembered his own feelings when he saw Cecilia's glasses on the bedroom floor. Then he knew he had to tell it.

"Enrico," he said, "I want you to listen to me."

The boy gave no indication of having heard him.

"Enrico?"

"Yes?"

"Tell me what happened to your father."

"What do you mean?"

"Just what happened."

"They came in the middle of the night and dragged him away."

The despair in Enrico's eyes made Carlos feel like a man on a tightrope over a river, but he did not hesitate.

"Tonight your father will hear footsteps in the corridor outside his cell. A key will turn in the lock and the lights will go on and he will put his hand over his eyes to shield them from the glare. When he takes them away he will see that one of the men has a tray of food and a carafe of wine. There will be a man he had not seen before in a colonel's uniform encouraging him to eat and drink. After he finishes the colonel will tell your father there has been a mistake. They realize that a professor cannot understand the government. All they want is for him to be more careful about what he says to his students. The colonel will leave then, and one of the soldiers will take your father down the corridor to a lavatory where he will be allowed to shave. Afterwards they will join two soldiers in a black car, which will take your father to your neighborhood, where he will be released. It will happen, Enrico, believe me. If not tonight, then soon."

Enrico left with a gleam of hope in his eyes. All night long Carlos imagined it slowly fading away to pain, disillusionment, and finally confusion over why he had told such a terrible lie.

The next day Carlos was talking to his colleague, Esme Palomares, when the children began arriving. As he pushed his glasses up on the bridge of his nose Enrico came out from behind the curtains and ran toward him laughing and shouting at the top of his lungs. He collided with Carlos and threw his arms around him.

"It happened, Senõr Rueda. The room and the lights and the colonel! Even what he said to Father."

The other children gathered around, and as Enrico told the story Carlos looked over the boy's head at Esme and Silvio. He said later that he had never been more frightened in his life. As the boy talked excitedly to his friends Carlos disengaged himself gently and went over to his colleagues. It was merely coincidental, he explained. Anyone could guess the layout of the cells, and the images of Raimundo Garcia, what he thought, obviously sprang from an overactive imagination. Silvio, the great pessimist, shrugged and disappeared backstage. Esme just looked at him. "No," she said finally, "it's more than that." Her words broke down the shaky edifice of reason and made him feel that he had crossed a border, entering a place he could not put a name to.

Carlos and I had arranged to see each other the next day at the Raphael. Since it was cold and rainy, and my apartment felt emptier than usual, I arrived a few hours early with the notion of enjoying the papers over a leisurely lunch. The place had become something of a second home, and I settled comfortably into my favorite booth against the wall with the pictures of sports heroes and artists, of Fangio and Borges, which always reminded me of the old, less complicated days.

I'd just finished one of the Raphael's famous steaks and started on a second glass of wine when I saw Carlos getting out of his Peugeot. Water was pouring off the awnings over the abandoned sidewalk tables, and when he passed through the sheet of water as if it weren't there I knew something was up. As soon as he came inside he took off his hat and edged his way through the tables to my booth. He sat down heavily, ordered a drink from the waiter who came by, and then looked at me with absolutely startled eyes.

"I don't know what to say, Martín, except that this is going to be hard to believe."

His voice quavered when he began telling me about Enrico and his father. He even spilled some of his drink before tossing it down in one gulp. I'd have been inclined to laugh at the whole thing if his fear hadn't become so palpable that I swear even now I could reach out and touch it. It was his body's conviction that made me realize he was serious. When Carlos talks his hands are in perpetual motion. I remember the arcs and the figures they made in the dim light, like sparklers carried by children at Carnival, and I followed them as if they were beckoning me into a strange place which I believed in and denied, all at once. It seemed to me that Carlos felt the same way, but when he got to the part where Raimundo opened his eyes I knew he was telling the truth. The occult lay there on the table between us, and we accepted it with no idea whether its meaning would be revealed. We did not broach that, nor did Carlos say a word about what his gift might mean for Cecilia. I didn't want him to, and I think that if he'd tried I'd have asked him to stop.

Then he was on his feet, ready to go, and I remember how he looked as he turned up his collar and went out into the rain. Perhaps it was just a trick of the lights at the Raphael, the yellow and red neon flashing off and on, but he appeared to move with a new authority, like a man who had suddenly discovered that he possessed something extraordinary. And I'll tell you something else. I hadn't the slightest doubt that Carlos would find a way to place his gift among the griefs of the city's people.

# 5.

A few days later he proved me right. The play he'd written for the Children's Theater was based on folk tales and required the children to learn an elaborate dance. After he and Esme blocked out the positions Carlos switched on a cassette recorder with a guitar piece, a passacaglia. The children took to it beautifully, moving in a series of figures which expanded and contracted in intricate variations. Some were in costume, others in street clothes, and as they danced it seemed to Carlos that they were multiplying like the cells of an embryo, the dozen children becoming scores of people from other countries and times. Suddenly, as if created by their energy, great white carnations blossomed and rose above the stage, white carnations with red and pink and golden centers, and in the heart of the largest a green Falcon bore down on the dancers and Cecilia, who had suddenly appeared. Surrounding her, moving in and out of focus, husbands and wives, daughters and sons, all calling for help. He did not understand that it was his help they clamored for. Only after straining to hear did he recognize his own name over the music, and its sound make him feel small and frugal.

Then the music ended and the children broke up into groups,

noisily debating what to do for the rest of the day. Lights blinked on and off at the far end of the aisles where some of them went out the front doors. At the table on the far side of the stage Esme and Silvio talked casually as Carlos looked around, almost convinced that Cecilia might be there. He said he felt as if he had a foot in two worlds, neither of which had the greater claim on reality. He did not know what would have happened if Esme hadn't asked him to join them for a drink. Her voice brought him back, and though he was grateful he offered a feeble excuse about having some errands to do and crossed to the steps leading down from the stage.

"Are you all right?" Esme called as he went up the aisle.

"Well enough," he answered, and continued without the slightest idea of where he was going.

He found himself driving on the belt road to the Paraná River where every car verged on becoming a green Falcon, every flower, garden, green space, or tree capable of blossoming into a white carnation. Long before he arrived he imagined that he could smell the river's muddy perfume, and he remembered the afternoons when he and Cecilia spent hours watching others who had also been drawn to its sedately moving waters. The memory made him dizzy, as if he were falling through himself, and he was grateful, when he arrived, for the families along the bank.

On the grassy knoll sloping to the water a man his own age sat with hands clasped on his knees, watching the river. Another lit his pipe, rose, and wandered off downstream. He heard a mother calling her son away from the bank, saw three girls chasing each other around a tree, tried to ignore two lovers lying on a blue blanket. It could have been ten years ago, and all of a sudden he was filled with anger at the people who acted as if nothing were wrong.

Every day a body turned up with a bullet in the head. Surely they had all heard of trucks coming to the river at night and the sound of a heavy splash such as a weighted body would make. Only a week before a woman crossing the bridge looked down and saw her husband floating on his back, like a starfish. She jumped in after him and drowned. How could they ignore the fact that even as the evening breeze came up someone was being taken from the streets of the city? But perhaps he only imagined their lack of interest. Perhaps the man with the pipe, now a tiny figure in the distance, wandered after an image of his wife, child, friend.

Carlos' anger vanished as he lay on the grass, his world reduced to the play of light among the leaves. He forced himself to watch the light and listen to the voices of the children, which sometimes rose above the splash of water. At some point the sound of the river became wind in a cave where, at the far end, Cecilia stood with the generals whose eyes brightened when they saw him. "Charm us," they said, "and you may have her back." He recited poems he had never heard, played strange melodies on an old guitar. Their faces softened. They conferred. Cecilia ran toward him calling his name and Teresa's, but as he reached out she disappeared. Only her voice remained, echoing some word he could barely hear over the water and the wind and then the word was gone altogether and he was listening to the screams of people falling from the sky and the concussion of their bodies striking water.

Every night Carlos dreamed of the images which came to him as he lay beside the river. Every day his imagination filled with the green Falcon emerging from the carnation, and through it all he felt his words gathering strength, becoming numinous. There was no longer a question of whether he would use them, but when, and that certainty brought a sense of peace which had eluded him since Enrico appeared, his father's salvation shining in his eyes.

We were at the Raphael when he told me about these things. He'd ordered a second Cinzano and turned it very slowly without taking his eyes off me. If you didn't know him you could have been excused for thinking he was slightly drunk when he said that his gift was like an instrument whose gold and silver strings made stories. There was a subtle change in his features as he spoke, as if he had truly come into possession of his imagination.

"I feel like I've returned from somewhere far away where old men with the voices of patriarchs instructed me in the use of the instrument, showing me how a sympathetic vibration between the strings annihilates distance so that the future and the past rush into the present. I know that sometimes the wires will break and the sound will be like a voice in a windy street. The instrument will be impoverished when that happens, but it is part of its life. If

34

I could I would place Cecilia inside, like a grain of sand which becomes the armature of a pearl, and put it away in a secret place. But those images at the theater, the people by the river, the dream that followed all mean I cannot hoard it for myself, or for Cecilia. I will lose the gift if I spend it only on myself."

I'm surprised by the speed with which both of us—two normal, intelligent men, accepted this deviation from reality. I didn't say understood it. In everything that follows Carlos never was any clearer about it than I was. I suppose it could be argued that we were predisposed to accept anything that might have the remotest significance for Cecilia. It would be only human, after all. But it's closer to the mark to say that a door opened, not unlike the door of the Mendoza's apartment, which unexpectedly revealed something that should not have been there. Put another way, our response wasn't altogether different from the peasant woman's who swore she saw the Virgin standing in the bow of a steamer from Germany as it made its way up the Río de la Plata, the difference being that she had only the proof of her own conviction, whereas Carlos' gift was manifested in a number of instances attested to by many people.

In any case, a little chill shivered up my spine as Carlos talked so calmly about the gift. He wasn't trying to find its essence in a metaphor, but actually describing how it looked. His eyes seemed very large and bright behind his glasses, which reflected the bottles on the bar. The pain was still there, but off a little to one side, as if making room for whatever was coming. In effect he'd told me he had made a decision, and that he was now searching for an opportunity to act. As things turned out, he didn't have to wait long.

# 6.

One Thursday, a few weeks after Carlos' vision beside the Paraná River, Esme returned to the theater from lunch and walked into his office without knocking. He was hard at work revising an intractable part of their script, and the interruption annoyed him.

"Carlos," she said, "there's something you have to see in the Plaza de Mayo."

"Can't it wait?"

"No," she answered, "some women are demonstrating."

"And nothing has happened?"

"Not while I was there."

Everyone knew the regime had banned public gatherings. Whether it was the result of a sixth sense on their part, or good intelligence, soldiers quickly surrounded even the smallest groups with jeeps and there were vans to take away anyone who refused to leave. Esme's news excited Carlos because he thought it might mean that a shift had taken place in the generals' thinking, and so he pushed the manuscript aside and grabbed his coat.

On the way out they ran into Silvio.

"We'll be back in an hour or two," Carlos said.

"What the hell is this?"

"I don't know, Silvio, but it's important."

The Plaza de Mayo was less than a mile from the theater on the most direct route from Carlos' house. Though it cost him an extra twenty minutes coming and going, he had avoided the area since Cecilia's disappearance because the Casa Rosada, the seat of government, lay just across the street from the Plaza. Carlos tried not to think about it as he and Esme walked along Avenida Victor Ruiz. All of his attention was on the obelisk rising from the Plaza, which was topped with the statue of a woman in flowing robes who carried a spear. They were still too far to see the circular promenade, and for a moment his eyes drifted from the obelisk to the spires and cupolas of the buildings beyond, the thrust of palms and jacarandas and palo borracho trees, the bell tower of the odd church. But when they crossed through the traffic of the round-about his gaze fell level with the Plaza where upward of fifty women were walking in a slow, ritualistic procession. Each wore a white scarf which bound them together in some as yet unknown sorority. Were it not for the scarves they could have been a cross-section of the city's women: some clearly middle class, who could have been his neighbors; some poor Indians whose skin shone like polished wood. They all carried signs so that at a distance they appeared like a gathering of religious zealots brandishing cryptic phrases from the Book of Revelations, advertising the apocalypse.

As soon as he and Esme reached the edge of the Plaza he understood that the signs were epitaphs and that the women were bound by motherhood. Photographs of the disappeared were centered in each sign, and beneath them were inscriptions written in large black letters:

WHERE IS RUBEN MACIAS?

WHERE IS JULIA OBREGON?

WHERE HAVE YOU TAKEN MY DAUGHTER

AND GRANDSON?

As the women moved silently past he could almost hear the anguish of their questions, but that imagined sound was less affecting than the faces of the mothers and those who'd vanished from their lives. It was as if life and death were joined in some strange rite, each feeding off the other. He watched, fascinated and

37

appalled, as the two orders of faces went by. Those of the distraught mothers mirrored the ghostly faces of young men, neatly combed and wearing their first suits, children posed self-consciously at holidays, a young couple holding a knife above a wedding cake, an infant in expensive clothes, a teenaged girl with a violin. They looked as lifeless as mug shots or passport photos. As Carlos was trying to understand what he saw he suddenly found himself staring at a picture of a woman who reminded him of Cecilia and then he was aware that Esme was holding his hand, though he did not know if he had reached for hers, or she for his. At that point he could avoid it no longer and turned north to face the Casa Rosada.

The windows set into its reddish stones appeared dead as black granite. As he tried to calm himself the venetian blinds behind the window at the far left-hand corner of the second floor were raised and a soldier leaned out and began photographing the women. The instant Carlos saw the telephoto lens everything became clear. The story about Enrico's father, the vision of the people on stage, Esme's appearance in his office less than an hour ago revealed what he had been looking for. He squeezed Esme's hand and said, "Wait here."

Twenty minutes later he returned from a stationer's at the southern end of the Plaza with a square of white pasteboard, a stapler, an ink marker, and a branch he had broken from a tree on the way back. As Esme watched he wrote in large black letters:

I AM CARLOS RUEDA.
THEY HAVE TAKEN MY WIFE.
I CAN HELP.

After stapling the sign to the branch he started toward the mothers. Esme caught his arm, but said nothing when he looked at her. When a space opened between a short, red-haired woman and one in a flowered dress he joined the procession.

Carlos walked with the mothers for the rest of the afternoon, long after Esme waved and left. No one spoke. Although the roundabouts were clogged with traffic, the accelerating engines and whining gears faded until he was aware of nothing more than the faint shuffling of feet in front and behind him. Whenever he turned north he imagined the whirring sound of the camera whose lens glinted in the sun, and then he elevated his sign and wondered if the generals were watching from behind the windows, opaque now with the sun's reflection.

They disbanded at dusk and some of the mothers gathered around him near a stone bench. They were shy and desperate and he thought he had seen them all on the stage of the Children's Theater.

# 7.

Carlos showed up at the Raphael a few days after Esme took him to the Plaza de Mayo, and when he mentioned the sign he'd made I thought it was dangerous and told him so.

"Why call attention to yourself?"

He answered that when he'd realized what he had to do it seemed essential to show the mothers that he was as strong as they were, otherwise they would ignore him.

"Don't you see, Martín, I couldn't hide behind their skirts."

"And what is it you think you have to do?" I asked.

"I'm going to have them come to the house and I'll try to find their people."

He spoke matter-of-factly, as if what he planned were no more unusual than going to a film, or the races. As he talked I was reminded of an evening I'd spent years ago at a hospital listening to a young man explain why he'd shot his boss. It appeared that the boss was an emissary of the devil who had wired the young man's apartment and embedded a listening device in his head in collusion with a dentist. For a moment, and it was just a moment, I wondered if Carlos had crossed into the same terrain until the undeniable fact of Raimundo Garcia's return relieved my distress. I realized that I'd allowed my skepticism to surface because I was afraid of Carlos' ability, afraid of what it meant, and hopeful at the same time.

I must have been lost in my own thoughts because when he asked me to come to his house the next evening everything seemed preternaturally bright. The prospect excited me, and that evening I stayed up late working on a stained glass project. I'd taken up the hobby years ago and the deliberate process of cutting the glass and fitting it into the lead cam moldings usually calmed me down, but when I went to bed the pieces floated around in my mind's eye and I dreamed of Carlos rearranging them into a fantastic pattern.

On Thursday night the city was even more beautiful than usual. At twilight our famous *porteño* sky becomes chrome yellow and then suddenly gives way to darkening shades of purple, as if a watercolorist were laying down washes to create a mood. The light was still soft and hazy when I arrived and Teresa let me in, saying that her father needed to be alone for a while and that I should make myself at home. I mixed a drink and went out to the garden where I found a place that would let me see the street through the iron bars of the fence.

People began showing up almost as soon as I'd sat down. It was clear from their faces that the very poor had walked in from *barrios* miles away. Others came up from the bus stop at the foot of the street, and soon a dozen cars were parked out front, Chevrolets, Renaults, Fiats, even a Mercedes. When the yellow halogen bulbs hanging from the metal stalks of the lampposts came on, the tiled roofs and white walls of the houses across the way seemed to shrink, and I remember feeling that sudden sense of isolation very strongly.

The light in front of the Ruedas' house illuminated wrought-iron lacework in a gate opening into the courtyard where a brick walk led around the left side of the house to the garden which was always redolent with the scent of cyclamen and roses. It was Cecilia's garden, I mean she was the one who designed it, potted the plants, tended them. She was almost always working there when I came to visit and that night I was more deeply aware of her than I had been in weeks, as if the garden were part of her, an extension of the woman who created it. At any rate, I felt the

41

connection very keenly as I watched the people cross the flagstone patio where an old pepper tree dropped red berries on a round bench covered with pots of star jasmine. Near it weathered rattan chairs were scattered around two iron tables painted cobalt blue and the mothers sat in them self-consciously, clearly ill at ease. Beyond them the garden ended in a stand of lemon and orange trees, a mimosa, and a plantain, which almost obscured the clay wall at the back. Pots of geraniums, azaleas, jade plants, and rosary vines surrounded the trees and topped the wall where an espalied bougainvillea showed blood-red in the light of lanterns suspended from the citrus trees.

Soon the garden was filled with young women, mothers, grandmothers, a few men, and three children. Since Carlos hadn't come out I went inside and found him in his study, a pleasant room simply furnished with two chairs, a desk, the sofa, two teak bookcases. A Guatemalan rug covered most of the tiled floor and prints by Picasso, Chagall, and Miró lined the walls.

He nodded when I told him the people were there but he didn't speak, only motioned to the sofa where I sat down and felt at loose ends because he seemed completely absorbed by some pictures of Cecilia on the desk. I could see her standing beside the plantain in the garden, looking humorously out of a portrait of the editorial staff at La Opinión, putting a gaucho's hat on Teresa at Carnival in La Boca. Her black hair and blue eyes were very clear, almost luminous, even at a distance.

Carlos stood up. He looked different from the way he had the day before when he spoke so confidently. The excitement was still there, but he seemed shaky, not uncertain, just a little off-balance and tense, the way I imagine actors get before going on stage.

"I was afraid it wouldn't work," he said.

"Cold feet?"

"No. After we marched I came back here wanting to blow up the Casa Rosada. I got over it and started thinking about tonight when I realized I didn't have any words. I mean I felt empty. Ten minutes ago I wasn't sure I could go through with it. When you came in I realized that I *don't* have the words, the people do; I mean they brought them."

He watched Teresa through the glass doors where she was finishing with the lanterns. Carlos was far away from me, separating himself as he prepared to go outside. I don't think I've ever had an experience like it. People get lost in thought all the time, but it was something more with him, not a ritualistic preparation, but like it. At any rate, he seemed to be speaking in a room with an echo when he said, "It's time," and I followed him outside where he sat in an old rattan chair facing the people and Teresa put a glass of tea on the wicker table beside him. I'd found a place in back, and as Carlos settled down and looked at the women I understood the feeling about him I'd had in his study. He reminded me of a heretical priest confronting a bishop who demanded an explanation of his strange behavior, something in the way of justification for returning from a place no one else had ever seen.

"Where shall I begin?"

No one insisted on being heard before the others, and I was touched by their politeness. They spoke quietly, in voices as subdued as the shadows of the lanterns on the flagstones. The first was a woman sitting next to me in a gray suit and heavy, gold-rimmed glasses.

"My son has been gone a month. He is an athlete, and never said anything about politics. They took him at the stadium."

Then a portly man with a drooping moustache whose shirt collar looked like wings.

"My wife's cousin, who lives in Bahía Blanca, is a *montonero.* My wife despises this cousin and thinks we should wait until things change by themselves. She told the police so when they came to our house, I mean that she hates her cousin, but they only laughed and dragged her down the stairs."

After him an old woman in a faded dress, one of those who had walked in from the city.

"I cannot bear it any longer. They took my grandson, Victor Madrid. He is only a schoolboy who sometimes says foolish things he does not understand. One morning he went to school and never returned."

"What is your name, señora?"

"Concepta Madrid."

"And what do you think will happen?"

"Ah, señor, do you have to ask?" Her voice caught, and she paused to regain control. "They will take my grandson somewhere and blow out his brains."

Carlos leaned back, fingers extended in a triangle to his lips. I could barely make out his eyes behind his glasses because of the reflection of the lanterns, but they looked diffuse and concentrated at the same time. He began to speak then, looking up into the trees as if he were describing something he saw there. To hear his voice that way frightened me and made the scene come alive all at once.

"As Victor said good-bye to his friends and left the school-yard a green Falcon pulled up to the curb. Before he knew what was happening two men had him by the arms and forced him into the back seat. One smelled of wine, the other wore a beret and sunglasses. Neither of them said anything as the car sped through the city, but within minutes Victor knew they were headed into the pampas and that they would kill him there. Although he was frightened, his thoughts arched back to the students at the Café del Sol, where he had spoken two weeks ago. Tristan could not have betrayed him. They had grown up together. Roberto was too timid. It had taken weeks to get him to come to the meetings. The beautiful girl in the corner was mourning a cousin who had disappeared. He saw everyone in the room and could not imagine whose voice led him to be pinned between the men.

"Victor saw a stop sign where the road curved into the high-way, and as they pulled up behind three trucks he swung his elbow into the throat of the man with the sunglasses and managed to open the door before he felt the pain in his skull and heard sounds like a brass band. His vision was like a kaleidoscope in which there were a dozen men. When it cleared the man was sitting up, holding his throat very gently with one hand. With the other he put his sunglasses on, and then he began striking Victor in the face with his fist while the man smelling of wine held him. They called him filthy names, and as the pain increased he thought about his grandmother and Maria Torres, who said she would marry him someday. When he remembered being with her in the Botanical Gardens where they went only a few days before it took all of his will power not to cry.

"After a while a eucalyptus grove appeared in the distance.

44

Victor knew that was where they were going as the car pulled off the road and passed half a dozen gauchos riding in single file in the tall grass. When the car stopped the men pushed him out and forced him toward the trees. Victor did not hear the gauchos bearing down on them, but the men did. Suddenly the air was filled with curses. The one with the sunglasses pushed him into the shade and raised his pistol. Victor heard a shot and saw part of the man's head fly off like a startled bird. Then the gauchos were there on horses huge as those in dreams. One pulled Victor up to the saddle, and as they rode off Victor heard shots but did not turn around. They rode for a long time before reaching an *estancia* where the rancher gave him wine and corn bread and told him he was safe.

"Last night Victor sat outside the bunkhouse with the gauchos. During the last few weeks he has gotten used to the pampas—he likes the way they look at night, and imagines that he can see the city's lights on the horizon and those imagined lights encourage him to think about his grandmother and Maria Torres. Tonight, at this very moment, in the neighborhood of Río Campo, a boy is bicycling past Number thirty-four, Calle Ventana Sur. He is singing a favorite song as he goes out of sight around the corner. In the alley he will prop his bicycle against a fence and go to the mailbox at Number thirty-four where he will leave an envelope for Concepta Madrid. 'Grandmother,' it says, 'I am safe. Tell Maria.' "

The name of Victor's fiancée floated in our imaginations, carried there like the emotions you feel after a musician plays the last chord and silence seems like an echo of the music. The sensation lasted for a long time. When it wore off, I felt as if I were standing in front of a magician's booth.

"I know what you think," Carlos said as he looked around. "You have to understand that we have left that place where everything is unchangeable. Give me more names."

It should have been a ludicrous moment. We should have seen Carlos as a charlatan with good intentions, but I believe everyone felt what I felt—that we were indeed in a place where anything could happen.

"Give me more names," he said, and the voices rose once again. He began to speak as wind tossed the mimosa and plantain,

45

rippling across the bougainvillea so that it looked like red water spilling into the garden. When the wind died his voice sounded louder, more authoritative, filling the garden with prisons, houses in the pampas, abandoned buildings near the port where people languished in cells, or screamed from torture. The door of a young man's room, who went to sleep wondering if he would die the next day, opened in the middle of the night and he found himself in Uruguay being guided to a sanctuary. In another story there was only pain, and I could not bear the sobbing of the girl's mother when the shot came.

An hour must have passed before Carlos sat back and drained the glass of tea. The people were afraid, torn between the pathetic safety of not knowing, and the desire to know. Carlos was shaken and said that all he could do was tell us what he saw. I don't know if anyone else noticed it, but there was something behind the sorrow he felt for the dead girl, another story, and then I knew he was thinking about Cecilia. A woman began to talk about her son, but Carlos rose and went to her, taking her by the hand.

"Forgive me, señora, I cannot listen any more just now. I must try to find my wife."

He went back to his chair and turned to Teresa.

"Tell us what happened."

Teresa's eyes were bright and uncertain—she hadn't expected this—and when she spoke her voice sounded as wooden as if she were reading a lesson at school.

"My mother is Cecilia Corazon Rueda. She was taken from our house by four men who came in a green Falcon. The neighbors saw them put her in the car. When Father came home the house was empty, but he knew something was wrong because of the *crudités* on the table. Her glasses were on the floor in the bedroom."

Carlos picked up the story as soon as Teresa's voice trailed off.

"This morning, on my way into the theater from the parking lot, I saw her walking by on Calle Onofro and I ran to the sidewalk where I grabbed her arm, but the woman who pulled away was a stranger. Inside I imagined her in the front row, in the seat she always took. It has been like that all day, even while we marched. Tonight I see her in your faces as she put the plate of *crudités* on the table and looked up when there was a knock on the door. As soon as she opened it and saw the men she ran to the bedroom and tried to close the door, but they pushed it open and in the struggle her glasses came off. In the car she looked back at the house the way near-sighted people do, and her face seemed like a papier-mâché mask of Fear I once designed and saw again today in the windows of the Casa Rosada.

"That is where Cecilia came to life for them. Within weeks her name rose from the ground floor to the second and the third and finally the fourth, where it entered the generals' imagination. From an anonymous woman they used to pass without a second glance on the street, or sat beside without noticing in restaurants, she became Cecilia Rueda, the leftist, and their imaginations began working on her as rapidly as she wrote on the old typewriter in her office. She had an identity then as one of the most dangerous journalists in Buenos Aires, a female Timerman.

"At the beginning of all of this she once said that the only way Argentina could survive was for writers to tell the truth. The world and the Church would intervene and force the generals into civilized behavior. But the world ignores us and the Church, you know about the Church. It was inevitable that she would write the story about the children of La Plata and fully come to life for the generals. It appeared in the morning edition, and by noon the generals were talking. One wanted to shoot her as she left the office, one suggested a car bomb, but the moderates argued that it was a delicate issue. The public might be aroused by such open violence against a woman. Their delicacy lead to a long discussion out of which orders finally emerged, and in the hazy sunlight of that warm afternoon a green Falcon came to Calle Cordova.

"There is an old building somewhere fitted out as a clandestine prison. It is large and dark, like a warehouse. A scent of packing grease lingers in the air. Cecilia was taken there and put into what seems to have been an office of some sort. Except for a mattress, the room was empty and dark, its windows boarded so that only tiny slits of light came in. The only sounds she heard were the guards walking back and forth downstairs. At night the foghorns. After examining the room and realizing there was no way out, her fear gave way to depression. She had no idea what was coming.

"Twice a day, once in the morning, and again long after the

faint light disappeared between the boards, a sergeant brought a bowl of soup and some dried bread. He would leave the door open so that she could see to eat, sometimes standing there watching her without saying anything, at others waiting outside where he talked to someone she could not see. On the third or fourth morning Cecilia was awakened from a dream about sailing on the Río de la Plata by the key turning in the lock. She pulled the blanket around her shoulders as she sat up and hoped there would be a large portion of soup because she was hungry. When the door opened she saw the sergeant and behind him two men, one who might have been in the car that came for her, but she couldn't be sure because they came inside quickly and shut the door. They waited until their eyes were accustomed to the dim light, and she tried to prepare herself for what she knew was coming. She hoped she'd misread the signs, but as soon as the sergeant said, "I've been feeding her, so I'm first," she knew. The two who came with him approached and took her by the arms. She moved crab-like away across the mattress, up against the wall, and then the sergeant struck her. "Make trouble and I'll do it again." Then they raped her.

"Afterwards she was dragged, weeping and hysterical, into another room and tortured with electric wires while someone asked questions very calmly behind her. This went on for days. Sometimes the same men came, sometimes not. When she appeared to be in danger of going beyond hysteria, only one came into her room in the morning. Then back to the other room where the shocks were more carefully administered. They asked specific questions about some cryptic phrases in her notebooks, which they found at our house. She resisted, lied, and then pleaded when they caught her in the lies and threatened to apply the wires again. Finally she signed something, disgusted by her weakness and unaware that no one can resist forever. Nothing was as important as stopping the men from raping her. If it had only been the pain from the electric shocks she thought she could have resisted, but she could not bear the men's hands on her body.

"She made the right decision, for after the confession the rapes stopped. She was left alone, and when the door opened the following morning and she pushed herself back in the corner, not recognizing the sounds she heard as coming from herself, as she pulled the blanket and pillow over her knees she thought she might be dreaming when the guard, a man she hadn't seen before, left the food by the door and went outside.

"Within a week she recovered some of her strength. Since arriving at the warehouse she was allowed one trip a day to the dirty toilet downstairs whose walls were covered with graffiti and old pictures of naked women. One evening the guard took her down and even let her close the door. She heard him talking to someone whose voice she recognized as one of those who raped her.

"When she was taken to the toilet during the time they were raping and questioning her Cecilia noticed that the concrete into which the bars were set in the windows looked as if it were on the verge of disintegrating. It had meant nothing to her then, but that night it was everything. She stood on the toilet and grasped one of the bars, which gave way soundlessly, the powder of decomposed concrete sifting down onto her torn dress. She grasped the one next to it, which also came loose, and when it did she began to cry, aware of how easily she might have escaped if she only had had her wits about her. Weak as she was, she knew this chance would not come again. The opening above the toilet looked like a mountain pass, and if she failed to pull herself up to the window she would not be allowed to come there again. She stepped on the water basin, which grated noisily as the men burst into laughter. Then she pulled herself up and climbed through the opening and dropped down outside into a storage yard lighted at the far end by a single weak bulb high on the wall. There was a gate at the other side of the yard, which was unlocked, and when she passed through she found herself in a back street where she followed the train tracks into darkness.

"She knew she was in La Boca, reasoned that if she could find a house someone might take her in. She walked like an old woman who had been ill, and soon the tracks were gone and the pavement gave way to cobblestones. It was then she heard the car and tried to run, but she was wearing high-heeled shoes and fell. The car pulled up beside her and then someone struck her in the face and kicked her in the side. Everything went white, but she did not lose consciousness. As the men pulled her toward the car she shouted "Carlos! It's Cecilia!" Then the doors slammed and the car sped off into the night, its tires making a heavy sound over the cobblestones."

I heard the hard, rubbery sound of the tires as clearly as if I'd been there on the sidewalk while the thugs beat Cecilia, a sound so awful that I wished Carlos would go on and say something that would make me forget it, but it was clear from the way he sat there looking at one of the lanterns that he was finished. Something had happened to his imagination as soon as he described Cecilia going through the gate. Until then his voice had been strong, even though each detail cost him some new pain, but when she was free the story suddenly lost its force, the details becoming sketchy as he obviously struggled to keep her in sight. By the time he brought the car into the picture I had to lean forward to hear him. He knew he'd lost the thread, and so did everyone else. Some of the women were crying. The success of Victor Madrid and the boy who escaped into Uruguay were all but forgotten.

The people left quietly, but they could have made as much noise as the crowd at a soccer match and Carlos wouldn't have heard them. I didn't know whether he wanted me to stay so we could talk, or leave him alone. Teresa looked like she was in shock, so I went over and sat with her. Since I couldn't think of anything to say, I suggested that the best thing would be for her to go to bed. She looked a little dazed and nodded, whispered something to Carlos I couldn't hear, and went inside. He watched her as if she were a stranger.

"I should go."

"I lost her," he answered, "just like that. I can feel where the place is, but I can't see it."

"Do you want to talk?"

"I don't know. You must be tired."

"Give me a glass of wine. I'll go after that. I'll call the taxi now."

I made the call while Carlos poured the wine and put the bottle back on the sideboard. All the lights were on in the house, but Carlos seemed like a man in a hotel he'd never seen. We went into his study where he picked up the picture of Cecilia and Teresa at Carnival. Then he put it down and pointed with his glass at Picasso's guitarist.

"Have you ever looked at this carefully?"

"No," I said.

"Sometimes I imagine music coming out of it, a melody of single notes, more like a flute than a guitar. A few nights ago I dreamed that it didn't have any strings. Cecilia was in the dream, and I could see her lips moving and knew she was telling me where the strings were, but I couldn't hear what she said. It was like that when I was talking about her at the end."

I didn't know what to say to him any more than I had to Teresa, so I put my hand on his shoulder and he smiled.

"Come on outside and help me with the lanterns."

We'd just extinguished the last one when I heard the abrasive horn of the taxi in the driveway. Carlos was at the far end of the garden. A bird of some kind had settled into the mimosa, but the horn frightened it and it flew off. Carlos watched it disappear and then seemed to be looking at the stars. He obviously didn't want to be disturbed. The Southern Cross was very clear, Orion burned blue and cold, and for some reason I saw them in the taxi all the way home.

Not being clairvoyant, I had no idea what was going on in Carlos's mind out there in the garden. The fact of the matter is that his imagination returned after I left. When he told me about it a few days later, he said something about the bird convincing him that it had come to lead him to the place he hadn't been able to see in his story.

Five minutes after I left he'd gotten into his car and headed toward La Boca, convinced the bird was just ahead of the car's lights. By the time he reached the road leading to the docks he felt a little foolish, but when he turned up a side street the Peugeot's lights reflected off some tracks in the middle of the road. They did not look like those in his story, but he followed them anyway, and for the next half-hour peered into dirty windows which must have given back a faint reflection of his haunted face.

He was about to give up when he turned into another street where, like a gigantic cobweb in the glow of a night light, a cyclone fence rose out of the darkness. It did not look like the one in his story—the dimensions were wrong, and the fence was too high, but when he saw that the padlock on the chain was open he went inside the yard. As soon as he passed through the gate a Doberman came snarling out of the darkness, steam rising from its muzzle rimmed with bared teeth. When Carlos took a step toward the gate the dog rushed, tore his pant's leg, and then backed away. Carlos knew that if he turned and tried to climb the fence the dog would be on him, so he slowly reached for the chain, the dog snarling louder and louder as the links rustled against the wire. When the chain was in his left hand he swung his right arm and the dog jumped and at the same time Carlos brought the chain down on the dog's skull. It howled as Carlos backed up to the gate and then it rushed again, but when Carlos raised the chain it made little yelping sounds and skittered away. Then he was out of the gate and slammed it just as the Doberman leaped and he felt its weight. Blood welled from the wound and he said the dog's eyes through the fence were terrifying. Its barking rose hysterically as he left and headed back to his car.

By that time he was exhausted and a headache was pounding behind his eyes. The café on the opposite corner was still open so he went in, thinking a beer might settle his nerves. Half a dozen longshoremen sat at the bar and he found a place next to one, ordered a beer, drank it off, and ordered another. The man next to him tossed down his schnapps and asked Carlos why he had come. When Carlos said he only wanted a drink before going home the man stood up.

"Why here?"

"I told you, for a drink."

The next thing he knew he was lying on the floor. The left side of his face was numb, and when he tried to get up he fell. The room was turning round and round and in the middle of it the man was being pulled away by two or three others. Carlos felt blood flowing from his mouth as the bartender helped him to his feet, said something to the men, and led him outside to his car.

By the time he turned into Calle Cordova the first light of dawn had touched the roofs. Teresa saw him coming up the walk and began to cry, but she had enough presence of mind to take him into the bathroom, wash his wounds, and get him a brandy. In the mirror his lips looked swollen enough to burst. He had not spoken to Teresa since she came running out of the house, and he wanted to comfort her, but when he tried to speak his lips felt like a razor were being drawn across them. He began weeping then, without any warning. It wasn't from the pain, he said, but from the sight of his bloody lips, which reminded him of Cecilia. He knew Teresa was frightened by his tears and he managed to say, "They hurt." Then he went to bed.

By that time the sun was up and filled the room with light. He knew he would sleep better with the blinds down, but the effort of getting up was beyond him, so he lay there feeling each pulse of blood in his battered lips and staring at the bureau at the foot of the bed and the pictures above it of the sea. His shirt was covered with his blood as well as the Doberman's, and there was no way to distinguish which of the splotches were his, which the dog's.

He said he had begun to relax and breathe regularly again when the stories he had told the previous night, and details from his misadventure in La Boca, began to get mixed up as the brandy took hold. He knew he had fallen asleep yet he was aware of the dreams, as if he were awake and thinking about them. He saw himself at the river dreaming of the cave and the generals and Cecilia running toward him. Then the sound of voices filled the air and the beat of helicopter blades grew louder as red and white navigation lights winked on and off like stars, illuminating people being pushed out the side door. They came down slowly, some running frantically in the air, and among the screams he recognized Cecilia's voice, and saw her falling slowly, slowly, her clothes coming off, dress, bra, and underwear floating like pieces of a torn parachute above the white body that disappeared into the river flowing quietly under the black sky. He did not feel the chill as he dove in and found himself walking along a cobblestone street. Flower pots, coffee cans, food jars filled with geraniums lined the sidewalk, giving off a pungent, earthy scent. A huge black spider clung to the wall beside a grilled window. Closer, the spider became a woman's shoe with a broken heel hanging from a scrap of leather. A single violet grew in the shoe, and as he reached for it an old woman came out of the doorway with a watering can.

"So you've come at last," she said, as if she were expecting him. "I put it on the wall in case she returned. I thought I should plant the flower."

He awakened late in the afternoon. The pain of his swollen lips was sharp as he sat up and looked into the garden where he thought he saw the black spider on the white wall. The fronds of the mimosa and plantain waved lazily in the breeze, like strands of kelp in the clear green water off the southern coast, and as he watched he tried to will them into the shape of swords which might somehow cut through the flagstones, the cobblestone street of his dream, cut all the way down to the cave, which seemed very cold and rimmed now with ice.

# 8.

You can imagine my shock when we met the following Monday for dinner at a little Italian café we both liked. I arrived first, and the waiter had just brought my drink when Carlos and Teresa appeared. People turned and watched as they made their way to the table. I couldn't blame them for their curiosity. Carlos' lips were swollen and purplish, almost negroid, and a fierce red welt on his cheek looked raw and painful. I was surprised he wanted to go out in that condition, more surprised that he'd brought Teresa, although I knew he was concerned about her. Only after he explained what happened the night he went to La Boca did I understand. He knew the search had been impetuous, and as he described the attacks by the Doberman and the longshoreman, the dreams, it was clear that he felt foolish and off-balance. Teresa listened carefully, and it was then I knew she was there to protect him from any criticism; I mean her presence altered what I could say, and Carlos knew it.

After dinner he invited me to his house for the following Thursday. "Yes, please come, Uncle Martín," Teresa added. I don't know if I'd have accepted if she hadn't been so anxious for my company. To put it bluntly, I was afraid Carlos would try to find

Cecilia again, and the prospect of another failure, of seeing her emerge from some terrible place only to be reclaimed, was more than I wanted to deal with. I agreed despite those misgivings because something in Teresa's voice, in her eyes as she waited for me to answer, said that she felt the way I did. After all, the three of us had experienced the same extraordinary shocks—Cecilia's disappearance, Carlos' discovery of his gift, the brief hope we'd all felt when he tried to summon Cecilia only a few nights ago. That such conjuring had entered our lives was bizarre enough, but it was then I realized how deeply involved we all were, how close in feeling, so it was no wonder that Teresa would feel safer, more secure, with my grizzled beard nearby. If being there could help her and Carlos, I could deal with whatever happened.

When I arrived at his house a few nights later there were three times as many people as on the first night of the stories, and many white scarves of the mothers of the Plaza de Mayo were scattered among the new faces. Carlos' reputation was spreading already, and there would be a time when people would wait outside on the sidewalk, unable to hear or see anything, wait without a chance of getting in, but find some comfort in just being near.

As I came through the gate I heard voices near the front of the crowd, but the words were indistinct. Teresa was standing near Carlos and smiled when she saw me. There was an empty chair on the far side of the patio and I made my way quickly across the flagstones. I'd been trying to listen to the people and hadn't paid much attention to faces, so you can imagine my surprise when I saw Silvio Ayala. I didn't know him well, and I was content to let it stay that way. On the few occasions when I couldn't avoid him at parties I found him insufferably boorish and couldn't understand Carlos' affection for the man. We nodded at each other when I sat down. Then I leaned forward to catch what one of the newcomers was saying. Her name was Felicite Barbazon and she was talking about her husband.

"He is only a minor politician and is always careful about what he says. Three weeks ago, in the middle of the night, the men came to our house. I saw Hector standing in the door in his pajamas. 'What did I say?' he asked. I tried to stop them, but they pushed me away and slammed the door. They were driving off by the time I opened it and looked out."

Dolores Ocampo followed with a story about her brother, who had joined the Army two years ago because they were poor and he thought he could rise in the military, but he did not have the heart to be a soldier. He had been assigned as a guard in one of the prisons, and objected when an officer told him to beat an old man. He told Dolores that he was afraid something was going to happen, that he felt trapped and vulnerable whatever he did. He was right. The next day he did not come home.

The voices of Felicite Barbazon and Dolores Ocampo sounded the same to me. I'm sure they did to Carlos too. As others spoke I noticed the same tone—not outraged or even angered but quiet and defeated—and the worst of it was my sense that they were all telling the same story. The names were different, the locations, but that was all.

While I was thinking about this a woman on the other side of Silvio stood up. She said she was María Márquez. Her white scarf looked bright and pathetic as she announced that her son had won a scholarship to the university. A few months ago he had presented a thesis on extremism to his professor and then he had disappeared a week later.

"His name, señora?"

"Octavio."

"What does he look like?"

"Tall and thin with eyes like an eagle."

She stood there waiting for Carlos to ask her something else. A full minute passed before she realized he was finished with questions. When she sat down Silvio muttered something under his breath I didn't catch, but it made no difference. All my attention was on Carlos as he leaned back, finding Octavio in the leaves of the mimosa tree.

"Professor De Anza's office was in a corner of the Philosophy building with large windows opening onto the courtyard. His books were neatly ordered behind glass doors, and there were pictures carefully chosen to complement the patrician feeling of the office. On the wall behind him, beside a landscape by a famous artist, hung framed photographs of the professor with politicians.

Octavio wished he could go behind the professor's desk and read the inscriptions on the pictures but he sat quietly and watched the professor flip through the introduction to his thesis and then drop it on the desk. Professor De Anza looked over the top of his horn-rimmed half-glasses and told Octavio he would read it soon and make an appointment to discuss the work with him. After Octavio left, the professor swiveled around in his chair and stared out into the courtyard. He took off his glasses and carefully polished them with his tie. As soon as the door closed behind Octavio he put them back on and began reading.

"He read without a break through the morning and into the afternoon, so absorbed by Octavio's ideas that he almost forgot his two o'clock lecture. Professor De Anza was one of the most unforgiving members of the faculty, and that afternoon he was more vitriolic than usual when a hapless student asked him to clarify an elementary point.

"Afterward, the professor retired to his office and continued with Octavio's thesis. With each page he grew more outraged at the boy's argument that the good citizen owed allegiance to his personal ethics and nothing else. Professor De Anza was outraged because he believed, with Plato, that we must obey the state, whether or not we accept its values, because the state is to the citizen as parents are to children. Anything less than total loyalty was treason in his eyes, leading inevitably to weakness, and even to the madness of anarchy. The professor could not believe that anyone who studied with him could be so deluded, and he took the polemic at the end of the thesis as a personal attack, a refutation of positions he had refined over twenty years.

"There was more to his response than the simple reaction of a bruised ego. During the week that followed he thought about what such ideas in one of his students might mean to the authorities, and how easily Octavio's views could be misconstrued as his own. Professor De Anza concluded sadly that the boy was a menace to himself, the university, and the state. Over the weekend he spoke to a friend in the government about Octavio. His friend commiserated. Disloyalty in one's students was truly shocking. Afterward, the professor's heart was heavy. Only a month before he had been forced to make a similar call about another student, the daughter of a friend. In the evening he went to a nightclub with his wife where he drank too much brandy and wondered if anyone there could understand the dangers posed to them by someone like Octavio Márquez.

"Monday morning, as Octavio approached the university gates, two men accosted him and minutes later he was on his way to the Naval Mechanics School. They passed uniformed guards at the gate, went up the drive which circled the neatly manicured lawn. Here and there a cadet strutted and watched the car. At the back of the building Octavio was led downstairs to a white room, very clean and bare. There, several other men came and forced him to remove his clothes.

"For two weeks he was kept naked in the white room where men beat him with hoses and subjected him to electric shocks which drained the current from the lights. Octavio could see the lights dim before everything went red and white. When live wires were applied to his testicles, he felt as if a hot vise had been clamped to the tenderest part of his body. After telling him he would never be with a woman again, the men forced his mouth open and applied the wires to his tongue because, they said, he needed to learn to speak with respect. This part of the torture was worse than what they did to his genitals because it seemed as if they had reached inside him. Each time the current surged through his mouth he could smell the smoke of his tongue. They did this every day until he did not even know his name.

"One morning Octavio was taken to a car where he was forced to lie on the floor. A man put his feet in the middle of his back. Some time later the car pulled over and the driver asked his companion to go in and buy cigarettes. As he got up he stepped on Octavio's hand, grinding his heel until the pain was so intense Octavio screamed. A minute later the car was moving again. 'Stay where you are,' the driver said.

"They drove for hours, and during that time Octavio tried not to think about what this meant. At the beginning tops of trees and the upper stories of buildings appeared in the rear window, but for some time he had seen nothing but a cloudless sky and he concentrated on it, forcing himself not to think about where they were going. Then the car was bouncing slowly over what must have been an unpaved road and finally came to a stop. He heard the driver get out and speak to someone before opening the back door and untying his hands. 'Come,' the man said. Octavio found himself in front of an old farmhouse where two men waited for him on the veranda. 'You are safe here. When you are better we will take you to a place where you will meet your mother.' As he tried to thank them his words sounded strange. He knew then that something terrible had happened to his tongue.

"Go home now, señora. In a while a man who sells fruit will come for you in his truck. Take what possessions you can, but hurry."

Watching Carlos tell the story fascinated me. Most of the time he kept his eyes on the mimosa tree, though occasionally he glanced at Maria Márquez, always with the same expression. At first I saw only defeat, resignation in her face, but as the story unfolded all her grief rose to the surface. You could tell that she almost believed Carlos was saying such terrible things to taunt her, to give her more pain, but the moment the car left the Naval Mechanics School something changed, surfaced. The tears and accusation in her eyes gave way to astonishment as the boy was led into the farmhouse. She believed, despite the fact that all she had before her were the images of Carlos' recitation. She rose and thanked him profusely. I had a desire to go with her and wait until the fruit seller arrived in what I suddenly imagined very clearly to be a delapidated Mercedes truck.

I might have gone if something hadn't intervened. I have said that I was surprised to find Silvio Ayala in the garden, and was not pleased to have to sit beside him. From the moment Carlos began Octavio's story Silvio shifted and sighed, his sense of his own superiority as evident in those gestures as if he were an atheist who'd gone to Palermo Park on a Sunday to debate the existence of God with a wild-eyed fanatic. I expected him to do something boorish, like interrupt the story with a fatuous remark. Silvio is like that. So you can imagine how I felt when he responded to Carlos' request for more names in a voice that sounded utterly foreign to everything I thought about him. Tall and thin, when Silvio speaks you hear the depth and resonance of a good baritone, a sound that suddenly had risen half an octave and had no more color than Teresa's voice.

"They have Rubén Masson. Sometime early this morning they took him and everyone in the family, even the baby."

Carlos did not say anything, but the muscles tightened in his jaw. He and Silvio and Rubén had all started at the Children's Theater and there was a crisis a few years ago when Rubén decided to become a filmmaker. Carlos and Silvio looked at each other across the white scarves a long time, Carlos silently urging Silvio to go on, Silvio caught between his habitual irony and the pain of what he needed to say.

"Tell me what happened, Silvio."

Silvio made a sound, a quick burst of air calculated to dismiss the whole thing as utterly fradulent, and he looked at me, quickly, his contempt for the process as clear as Maria Márquez's belief had been not three minutes earlier. I was amazed when I saw tears welling in his eyes. When he spoke, he seemed to be gasping for breath between every third or fourth word.

"There is almost nothing . . . to tell. When his secretary came to pick him up . . . the door was open . . . she went inside. The place was wrecked. She called Rubén, Marta . . . the children. She went up to the baby's room . . . found the crib . . . overturned."

Carlos didn't move, but his eyes slowly turned and focused on the lantern hanging from the mimosa. I don't know how long he looked at it. When he finally spoke it was in a tone I hadn't heard before, somewhere between Silvio's and his own when he'd first told me about Enrico Garcia.

"Rubén loves Antonioni's *Blow-Up*. 'Enlarge anything enough,' he told me once, 'and you see the evil which has always been there.' It was the same in Rubén's life. A few days ago he asked one of his actors if he were interested in making a film about the disappeareds. Of course they would do it secretly and smuggle the print out of the country. After the day's work was over the actor, Dario Montalban, went to his mistress's apartment on Avenida Corrientes, and while she made drinks he placed a call on the phone in the bedroom. He got through on the third try. The woman felt rejected because he'd hardly said a word to her, and

Dario found it necessary to take her to a good restaurant in Calle Florida. Rubén knew nothing about this. All he knew was that when the police came this morning Darío Montalban cast a huge shadow on the wall in the living room, a shadow which grew until the head and shoulders spread along the ceiling and seemed to encircle everyone in the room.

"It is always difficult with families. Things work best when one of the Falcons pulls quickly up to the curb and someone is dragged inside. For families they dispatch black paneled trucks with the insignia of the post office emblazoned on the doors. Those who drive the Family Buses, as they are called, wonder, over beer and calamari, if they might find an old Nazi who still remembers how the mobile vans worked.

"As they were pushed into the van Marta and the two little boys, Roger and Joaquín, were crying. Roger tried to get out and one of the men picked him up and threw him back inside. He wasn't hurt, but Rubén almost wished he had been because physical pain would have been easier to bear than the terror in his son's eyes. By the time the doors were slammed the baby, Felicia, was screaming, and the sound enveloped them like Dario's shadow had minutes before. Rubén could not say anything, only cursed himself silently for having proposed the film as he reached out in the dark and pulled them all together. They huddled on the floor, arms around each other, as the van made its way through the streets they could not see.

"They are in the Naval Mechanics School and Rubén does not know that he will never see Marta or the boys again. He will be tortured over the next few days, asked questions that do not make sense. He will soon be willing to tell them everything about his film, but when he tries to speak he will only babble. They will leave him alone for a while, and just as the pain recedes enough for him to think, when his eyes stop jumping around, he will hear Marta's voice and think he will go mad if she does not stop screaming. The room where he is kept has no windows, the door is solid, the walls thick, but not thick enough to prevent the sound from seeping through. He will not know whether she is somewhere beyond the wall to the left or the right. When she screams again he yells her name, demands that they stop. The only answer will be her screams, which he thinks contain a recognition of his call, and then he thinks he can hear their voices echoing together in the hallway they walked along only a few days ago. He will not know what to do except to continue to yell her name as he unthinkingly swings his fist into the wall, greeting the pain like an anesthetic.

"The next day there will be no more screams from Marta. Rubén will not have time to think about this because they will torture him again. He will try to see the boys and the baby and Marta before the pain comes like lightning from the rubber hoses and the light explodes like fireworks when the current is turned on. He will vanish into the pain, ignorant that Marta died the day before because the voltage stopped her congenitally weak heart. He will not know what happens to the boys. All he will know is that he is breathing, that the torture has stopped, and that sometime later, a day or a week after being dragged back to the cell, the door of his room opens and Felicia is dropped into his filthy lap.

"Then he will know that Marta is dead. He will lean against the thick wall with Felicia in his arms knowing that when they come again they will do something unspeakable to her. He wonders if, while he still has the presence of mind and strength to do it, he should kiss the baby and put his hand over her face. He imagines the brief struggle, the body stiffening and going limp, the agony of not being able to do the same thing to himself. But by then Felicia has stopped crying and is sound asleep. Rubén will hold her and look around the room, measuring the thickness of the door and walls. It will be very quiet and Rubén will stare at the wall all day, and he will continue to stare, even after the feeble light has been turned off. He will stare because there is nothing else he can do, because if his eyes stray from the invisible point of focus he will see what happened to Marta and Roger and Joaquín. And then a pinpoint of light will appear on the wall. He will think something is wrong with his vision until it grows larger, jagged. In a while moonlight will penetrate the opening in the wall, which will soon be large enough to crawl through holding the baby close. Outside he will wrap Felicia in his tattered shirt and then they will vanish in the night.

"I am not certain how long it will take, but Rubén will make his way to Brazil. He will survive and see Felicia grow up."

There was not a sound in the garden when Carlos finished. I don't remember anyone moving for a long time, as if the terrible story had deprived them of strength and volition. Silvio was sitting with his legs spread, hands on his thighs, staring at the flagstones, midway between despair and rage. Then one of the mothers got up and walked woodenly out the gate. Others followed, and soon only Carlos and Teresa and Silvio and I were left. Silvio looked at Carlos, who was not looking at anything. I could tell he was exhausted, asked if he wanted some brandy. He nodded and I turned to Silvio. "You too?"

"I don't want brandy. I want to talk to the magician."

Carlos did not seem to mind the sarcasm, but I wasn't sure because I went inside and all I heard before closing the door was Silvio telling him that he hadn't known what to do. Coming to the garden was all he could think of. "How can you say these things? It's obscene!" That was when I closed the door and saw Silvio laugh at Carlos' response. It looked as if he said "absurd, coincidence." For the next twenty minutes I made small talk with Teresa while looking outside every once in a while at Silvio railing at Carlos and Carlos calmly responding.

I wanted to help Carlos, even though I had no business doing it. I knew Silvio was ripping into him because of his grief and inability to accept what was, admittedly, preposterous on the face of it, but I took it personally because I knew Carlos' only defense was to tell Silvio something he didn't believe. If Carlos could have seen further into the future he might have found some help in Timerman's notion that what we had to deal with was the regime's desire "to ignore the complexities of reality, or even eliminate reality." But of course at that point Jacobo was still in prison.

Twenty minutes later they came inside. Nothing had changed. I knew that Silvio would continue to be abusive even though Teresa was there, so from my perspective there were only two choices. Everyone could go home, I said, or we could continue at the Raphael. I hoped Silvio would have the grace to leave, but he didn't.

We found a sidewalk table, ordered drinks, and sat there with the tension building, no one willing to break the silence. I actually felt sorry for Silvio. If anything, he looked worse than he did at Carlos' place.

We continued like that until some officers strolled by, and then a Falcon, bristling with aerials, cruised past so slowly that we could see the men inside looking us over.

"Do you know what they see, Silvio?" Carlos said.

"I suppose you'll say nothing."

"Sheep and terrorists."

Silvio looked at me and laughed. "What's that supposed to mean?"

"They see sheep and terrorists because they imagine us that way. But look at the people, Silvio, that old woman, the man in shirt sleeves. They remember a time before the regime, but they do not take their imaginations beyond memory because hoping is too painful. So long as we accept what the men in the car imagine, we're finished. All I've been trying to tell you is that there are two Argentinas, Silvio, the regime's travesty of it, and the one we have in our hearts. What do you think the mothers imagine in the Plaza de Mayo? The grandfather at Auschwitz as he watched his family marching toward the showers to the tune of Mozart's *Magic Flute?*" Last week I went to the Riachuelo to find a leather bag for Teresa's birthday. In one stall I discovered a lacquered bamboo cage in which two Amazon parrots perched lifelessly. Just then the woman who kept the stall unlatched the door and the parrots flew out. I don't know why she did it but that's what imagination can do, Silvio, fly like the parrots as they arched into the sky where they caught the scent of the jungle and rode the free air back to where they belonged. We have to believe in the power of imagination because it is all we have, and ours is stronger than theirs."

Silvio's arrogance had vanished. He was not even angry, and I think that was because he recognized the strength of Carlos' conviction. And yet his next comment made it clear that he could not accept what he couldn't see.

"But, Rueda, none of this stopped the people from being led into the showers."

Carlos looked very intently at him.

"How do you know?"

Silvio began to speak, but whatever it was got lodged. Did he see something? I don't know. The question held us silent for the next twenty minutes until he said he had to leave. He was hurt and troubled and I had no idea what Carlos' words meant to him.

On the way home I asked Carlos what he meant in referring to the camps.

"There was just an image, very clear, very precise, of an old man bereft of everything but his dignity. He could easily have sung a prayer for the dead. He probably did. But it is just as probable that he imagined a last-minute reprieve. For some reason the doors could have closed, the last people in line sent away. The question is whether his hoping, his imagination, had any actual effect, and there is no way for us to know, is there? I mean it could have been a simple matter of logistics—too many people—or temperament, or any number of things. Would it have happened if the old man had not sung his song? Probably. Could the miraculous turning away of his family have occurred without his imagination? I would be the last to presume an answer."

By that time we'd reached my apartment. I asked him in for a nightcap, but he shook his head.

"I'm tired, Martín. All I want to do right now is sleep."

Then, out of the blue, he said he was going away for a week.

"I decided a few days ago. Teresa can stay with Cecilia's cousin."

"Where to?"

"South, the pampas, maybe further. I know Cecilia's been in the city, in the warehouse, or someplace like it. I don't think I'll find her, but I'll find something. I'll call when I get back."

I sat up for a while, made some warm milk, and turned on the radio. They were playing tangos and the words expressed my own discouragement. I wished Carlos could let himself give up. As the music filled the room I looked out over the city whose lights were very bright and clear. I knew Cecilia was dead, and knew too that Carlos would have to discover it for himself. I only hoped that I would be strong enough to help him when the realization came.

# 9.

Much as I loved Carlos, I wasn't sorry he'd decided to leave the city for a while. For weeks my life had been complicated by ideas everything in my experience opposed. I thought I was too old to change intellectual habits, but my involvement with Carlos forced a radically new perspective on me. I've admitted to its fascination, but it was also wearing me out. Irony has always seemed the best approach to life, the best way to keep it at arm's length. My reputation was made as an ironist, and without warning I'd been transplanted to a sphere where my usual habits of thought were not only out of place, but inappropriate. You see, though I never liked Silvio Ayala, I understood him because his was only a more skeptical version of my own position. Carlos' extraordinary gift hadn't converted me to optimism, though it gave new meaning to the concept of wonder—even belief—which Silvio hadn't been able to share.

And so my old life welcomed me again. Even when I worked for *La Opinión* part of my daily routine included walking, and since my retirement I sometimes spent two or three hours wandering through the city. I walk because I love the place, because it is always the same and always different. I've never felt that way about Paris or Berlin or Copenhagen. Looking at a street, or at a park in the distance, reveals urban geometry that is more or less the same everywhere. But enter the street, the park, the subway, and Buenos Aires unmistakably summons you: Pavements, facades, iron gratings, water of innumerable fountains. A lone man smokes thoughtfully in the shade of an awning, a woman walking a dog suggests wonderful mysteries. Pigeons spring from unsuspected places and even laundry flapping from windows or lines on rooftops has a personality. I loved the spicy scent of corner groceries, the sight of men on the steps of streetcars, a butcher bent under half a beef carcass, the neon lights, the tramps, the young couples pressed close in the dark entrance of an apartment building, the clean white shape of subway cars. And when I was tired I could always stop for a drink in a strange café, or read papers in the National Library.

One Thursday I found myself, quite by accident, near the Plaza de Mayo, and since I'd never seen the march I joined a few other spectators. None stayed long, and I knew that was because what they saw didn't fit their sense of the dramatic. They left because there were no fiery speeches or soldiers rushing in to break up the procession.

The absence of soldiers eloquently testified to the confidence of the men inside the Casa Rosada that the mothers made no difference. They were the Crazy Ones the co-opted papers sneered at, parents of criminals or perverts. Over the years I've written about almost everything of interest in Buenos Aires. The one thing I avoided—because there was no reason to deal with it—rose up before me like a physical presence, as solid and real as Kilómetro Cero. It was the insularity of the spectators, the shopkeepers, clerks, the elegantly dressed doctors and lawyers whose moral lassitude allowed them to find nothing compelling in the silent women. They knew what was happening and by turning away accepted it. Oh, there was concern in their eyes, even some sympathy, but what the mothers stood for would not interrupt their dinners later on, or affect their work, or keep them from the races at the Hipódromo, or the music at the opera. So long as it was not personal it had no effect. As I watched them leave I wanted to tell them some of Carlos' stories, describe what these women looked like in his garden when his powers couldn't change things, though I knew it would make no difference. Standing there, I had the distinct impression of seeing people hiding inside themselves, and I realized that my sense of the city's accessibility was false. I had seen its gestures, heard its voices, but it kept much to itself and I did not want to know that part, the way you would rather not hear about a lover's past.

A few days before Carlos returned from the pampas I had lunch with an old friend, Eugenia Rosas, in her apartment high above Corrientes. Her granddaughter, Maresa, was there, and it was very pleasant to hear her young voice and see Eugenia fresh from the beauty shop. I felt centered, part of an establishment, the way I used to with Carlos and Cecilia. Maresa went off to meet some friends after we'd eaten and Eugenia sat down beside me, gave me a kiss on the cheek, and asked what was wrong. She is infallible in such matters, so I told her that I hadn't been right since the afternoon in the Plaza. Up to then I hadn't talked to her about Carlos because it seemed too strange. When I finished I said, "I'm seventy and can't accept a basic fact of human nature, of Argentine nature, at any rate."

"Oh, Martín," she answered, "you miss what's right under your nose. We aren't different from other people. Everyone's afraid, including those in the Plaza. Why do you think they left?"

From a certain point of view I could understand Eugenia's sympathy, but it seemed sweetly naïve soon after I left and I remained discouraged by the mothers' isolation. An aspect of our national character had popped up like the evil figure in a puppet show when I'd visited the Plaza de Mayo. And while I felt indignant about the cowardice of my fellow Argentines, I did not exempt myself from criticism. After all, the pieces I was writing for the French journal were under an assumed name. Of course, it would have been foolish to use my own—if that had been the case I'd have soon become the subject of one of Carlos' stories. The point is that I was not willing to commit myself, not any more than the people who turned away from the procession in the Plaza.

Given what I know about myself the disillusionment that sprang from my encounter with the spectators could easily have eroded the optimism I'd begun to feel. Fortunately Carlos returned from the pampas with a story so rich in hope and strength as to banish forever from my mind the notion that we were helpless and doomed whenever the generals strode toward us, their medals gleaming in the sun.

# 10.

He had only the vaguest sense of the geography of the pampas. His map showed several routes running south into Río Negro Province, and he decided arbitrarily to go as far as Viedma, though he did not rule out the possibility of continuing into Patagonia.

For most *porteños* travel in the pampas means going from Buenos Aires to Mar Del Plata or Bahía Blanca on the coast, inland to Santa Rosa and Neuquén, which is to say that the romance of the plains is almost exclusively something for export—for us they are barely more interesting than the industrial north of England to Londoners, the Bad Lands of America to New Yorkers. The pampas are only a spatial interlude to be traversed as rapidly as possible, a vastness whose horizon either frightens or bores, depending on temperament, and people drive all day without seeing anything but a continuum as undifferentiated as the sea to a sailor who has been away from home too long. When the hot pampero wind blows the wheat into whitecaps they wonder how people in the *estancias* along the way endure their isolation.

There is nothing wrong with such feelings. I have gone into the pampas myself on a few occasions and felt exactly like these travelers, but Carlos was not like us, and he set out in a much different frame of mind. He was not going anywhere in particular; rather, he was searching for something he could not even name, so the condition of his mind was necessarily different from ours— attuned to indistinct possibilities.

The land presented itself like a blank sheet of paper to his instincts, as if he were a Spanish cartographer in the early nineteenth century sent out by the administration to explore the forbidding sea of grass, a man who might instinctively turn away from the sun at midday and come upon an uncharted river, or a settlement. Carlos remembered old maps with delicately shaded mountains in fine brown lines of faded ink, grasslands with green tufts, like those a child would draw, streams appearing out of nowhere and vanishing into the tufts, arroyos, water holes, and wide expanses of thornbushes. Only a few hours away from the city he forgot its modernity and the arrogance of its buildings. He could have been on horseback, perhaps with a few underlings to provide protection should they encounter people living in grass huts and practicing a life utterly remote from the bustle of the settlement a week's trek behind them on the Río de la Plata. His own discoveries were modest: a hawk gliding on thermals, its body attuned to the slightest movement of prey in the grass and wheat. As the day grew hotter, a mirage settled over the land out of which emerged a herd of cattle, an owl, ovenbirds, and later a lone gaucho riding far off near the horizon.

Around noon he stopped for gas and something to eat in a settlement called Jolón. Back on the highway, he let himself be lulled by the heat. Time passed without a thought. He did not know how long he had been driving since leaving Jolón, but the sun had descended, shining like an orange disk in the rearview mirror so that everything behind him was bright and luminous, while ahead the land blurred into shades of purple and the road lay out flat and dark. The fading light encouraged misgivings about his adventure. He thought that he might drive all the way to Tierra del Fuego without anything happening to him when he saw three giants striding across the wheat toward a line of diamonds which soon became windmills and lights of a town. He stopped at the Hotel Bella Vista and took a room on the second floor. After unpacking he had a drink sent up and sipped it as he looked out the window at the lights of two cars on the highway which quickly disappeared, taking with them all sense of space. As he went downstairs he felt as if he were still on the road with the wind whistling in his ears.

He found a café at the edge of a square between the church and municipal building. Lombardy poplars and blossoming acacias leaned over tables spilling onto the square. Inside, an accordionist played tangos while two couples danced raggedly. The walls were covered with posters advertising races of three seasons ago at the Hipódromo, in Buenos Aires.

Carlos took a table between an old priest and the musician. When the proprietor bought the spiced beef and coarse bread Carlos noticed that one of the gauchos at a table near the door was staring at him, but he finished his dinner and drank the last of the wine without looking up. As he was about to leave the man and two others rose and came his way. They were dirty, and the one in the lead looked as if he hadn't shaved in two or three days.

"Forgive me, señor, I am Domingo. I saw you come in."

Carlos introduced himself and said that he'd come from the city.

"To visit our town? Why would we interest you?"

"I'm just passing through."

"To where?"

There was an edge to Domingo's voice, though he seemed neither rude nor threatening.

"I don't know."

"Nobody drives in the pampas for pleasure. I will tell you what I think. I think you are the police and we do not want you here."

Carlos laughed. It was the last thing in the world he thought he'd be accused of.

"I think my wife might be here," he said, and then briefly told them what had happened.

"I understand," Domingo said. The tension had quickly gone from his voice. "My nephew also disappeared. He had only been in Buenos Aires a month and nobody knows what happened. Sometimes a body turns up in the grass. They say some people escape,

73

but I don't know. It is very big, this pampas, even if she got away, the heat, and no water . . ."

They had some more wine and no one mentioned Cecilia or Domingo's nephew. When they left Carlos wondered why they believed him so readily. It was midnight by then, and except for the accordionist drinking at the bar and the priest and proprietor, the café was empty. The priest nursed a drink and occasionally scribbled in a notebook. As Carlos left the priest took a manuscript from a worn leather folder and began entering the notes, oblivious to everything and clearly at peace.

The next day Carlos felt the size and unreality of the pampas. The excitement of the first day had worn off and now that he knew about the mirages, the way animals and fences and strange objects exchanged identities as they were melting, he settled back and let the heat play over him. From time to time an *estancia* turned up in the distance, but he saw nothing that made one different from the others. The names of the places—Twenty Acacias, Sweet Water, The Brothers—blurred together. All morning and into the afternoon he drove with only the vaguest sense of Cecilia.

He had taken the Peugeot up to one hundred and twenty kilometers in order to have something to concentrate on when a line of poplars caught his eye. The land had been slowly changing and it was definitely greener now. There were rises, almost hills. The poplars began at the top of a rise and descended in neat lines. Carlos slowed down to see what lay beyond them when suddenly a flamingo flew low over the grass. The bird rose and turned toward the poplars where Carlos saw the tiled roof of an *estancia* through the trees. He pulled off the highway into the gravel lane running up to the house thirty kilometers away. Across the lane a sign on a fence post named the place ESPERANZA, and below it the owners, Amos and Sara Sternberg. All the way down the lane birds flew in and out of the trees. Three or four flamingos sailed above the tops, while parrots and macaws and cockatoos dove and glided and turned below them like details in dreams, or surrealistic paintings. Just then three Argentine goldfinches settled on the Peugeot's hood. Two walked back and forth before settling down to preen themselves, but the third came up to the windscreen and looked at him, turning its head back and forth, as if to check the

74

image of one eye with the other. A minute later the finch rose and flew around the car half a dozen times before heading off down the lane. Carlos put the car in gear and followed it without a second thought.

The lane led to a circular drive surrounding a teardrop of lush grass, and when the poplars no longer screened the place he saw that only the upper part of the house was white: the area from the windows down was painted red, green, and blue, sharp primary colors, like the birds. A veranda extended the length of the house and along the edges, as well as from the eaves, pots of fuchsias and begonias were painted the same colors as the house.

On a bench at the far end of the lawn in the shade of some acacias a man fed parrots, macaws, and dozens of goldfinches, which spiraled down from the trees, taking seeds from his hand and flying back up into the branches. Two parrots came over the drive and landed on the back of the bench, sitting like patriarchs, watching Carlos as he got out of his dusty car.

The man rose and put the packet of seeds in his pocket. As he came out of the shade he raised his left hand in greeting, while in the other he held a cane and leaned on it heavily as he crossed the lawn. His long gray beard set off blue eyes, which even under a slouch hat were clear and curious. When he reached the gravel drive he smiled.

"Welcome to Esperanza. You are either lost or dying from the heat, or is it both?"

A parrot landed on his shoulder, stared at Carlos.

"This is Ephriam. Forgive his bad manners. He has been like this all his life. And my manners, too. I am Amos Sternberg. Come and have something to drink."

A woman came out and shaded her eyes from the sun. She seemed to be studying Carlos, and he had the feeling that she had been watching from inside.

"My wife, Sara."

She was about Amos' age, in her early seventies, and like him deeply tanned so that the gray hair, which was pulled back in a bun, appeared even whiter. She was remarkably beautiful, but he could not reconcile her beauty with the white caul of a cataract on her right eye. Her presence seemed defined by that single flaw,

75

which gave her an orphic quality. Amos went inside and Carlos heard him speak, but he did not know if there were more birds in the house, or another member of the family. He felt shy with Sara and did not say much until Amos returned and they settled with their iced tea into some cane chairs.

"So what brings you here?" Amos asked.

The surprise of seeing the birds wheeling through the trees had made Carlos forget Cecilia. Amos' question brought her back, and with his consciousness of her a sense of the ludicrous. They would think him mad if he explained what forced him out of the city the day before. He thought about lying, making up anything that sounded remotely plausible, and he was about to say he was on vacation when he realized that for some reason he could trust them with the truth. He wanted to tell the story in a few sentences, but he found himself explaining everything very slowly. With each word, each remembered image, he experienced a sense of relief that was greater than when he talked either to me or Teresa. Whenever he looked at them they seemed to know what he was going to say.

After he finished he looked out at the grass where three flamingos were poised, motionless, near the bench.

"So that is why I've come. I'm sorry to bring such things to a place like this."

Sara leaned forward so that her elbows rested on the table as she turned her glass with her fingertips. It was streaming with beads of condensation.

"Carlos, what if you cannot find her? Have you thought about that?"

"I will."

"Is that just hope?"

"I do not distinguish between hope and belief."

Something happened then, though Carlos said he had no idea what it was. The best he could do was to tell me that there was a recognition on their part. Sara reached over and patted his hand as she quickly glanced at Amos.

"Stay the night. We can have dinner and talk later on. I'll tell Sasha," she said to Amos. "In the meantime, why don't you show Carlos around? He might like to see the lake."

Amos led him behind the house and past the outbuildings where some gauchos were working. They entered a thick stand of poplars and eucalyptus and the temperature seemed to drop ten degrees. They walked for upward of a kilometer before coming out of the trees where, beyond the cardoon and thistles and bulrushes he saw a small lake fed by a marsh-like stream at the far side. Half a dozen flamingos waded in the shallows, and in the shade of the grass there were herons and spoonbills and other birds Carlos did not recognize. Amos said there were other places like this in the pampas, though not often on private land.

"We are very lucky," he added.

On the way back they stopped to inspect some brood mares. Amos did not ask Carlos anything more about himself and Carlos felt even more strongly that there was some kind of shared knowledge between them, and that Amos was biding his time.

Sara was nowhere in sight when they reached the house. Amos said that she always napped through the afternoon heat and that it would be a good idea for them to do it, too. He showed Carlos to a clean white room and as soon as he lay down he went to sleep.

He woke an hour later refreshed and curious. There were voices on the veranda, and when he went outside the table had been set for dinner. The long twilight of the pampas had settled over everything. Beyond the lawn there was nothing but a purple haze. Amos gave him a glass of wine and they talked for a while about the horses he planned to show in one of the auctions. Sara came out with a tray, followed by a woman of about fifty carrying another one. Carlos assumed she was their daughter, though he could not make out any resemblance between them. She was fair, in fact her skin looked translucent in the light, and he thought she might be ill. She glanced quickly at him as she put down the bowls of soup and it was then, when her sleeve was pulled up, that he saw the tattooed numbers. She seemed to be wearing a flesh-colored mitten on her right hand, and only when he looked more closely did he see that her fingers were fused together with scar tissue.

Sasha did not appear again until they finished dinner, and

then only to clear away the dishes. When she went inside Amos lit a cigar and exhaled a cloud of blue smoke.

"So you see that some things intrude here."

"She's your child?"

"Sasha is the daughter of an old friend. Forgive me for not introducing you, but she is shy with strangers and prefers to eat alone when we have guests. You see, she cannot speak. After the Germans finished with her she became ill and offended a guard by asking for something to drink when she had a fever. He cut out her tongue with a bayonet and threw it in a refuse heap where a rat appeared to run off with it to his burrow. Sasha tried to follow but fainted from loss of blood. The guard was greatly amused. When she came out of the infirmary weeks later he was waiting at the door and asked if she were still thirsty. Do you see now that we understood what you told us earlier?"

A parrot settled onto the railing of the veranda and Amos gave it a few seeds from his pocket.

"We lived as you do now for years. When it was all over the first thing I asked the Russian sergeant was the day, year, time: 27 January 1945, 3 P.M. Next to our wedding it is our most important date. The sergeant took pictures, and I asked if he would send prints to me care of my cousin in Argentina. I didn't believe him when he said he would, but they were here when we arrived a year later."

Amos went inside and returned with some faded pictures of the barracks. There were also two pictures of people with no hair who looked like skeletons, and one of the skeletons standing next to each other, either crying or laughing. Amos nodded when Carlos looked up.

"At the relocation camp the doctors tried to do something about Sara's eye, but it was too late. We were there for months before we really believed we were free. Our town in Poland had been leveled, but even if it hadn't we knew we could never live in Europe again. We thought of Israel, even made plans to go, but this estancia has been in the family for a hundred years and my cousin died during that period, leaving everything to us. Even now it seems miraculous. Some people think the pampas is too empty, but I say that I can see in all directions."

"How did you survive?"

"We survived because we knew we were not what you see in the pictures."

Amos sipped his drink.

"What do you see in those?" he said, pointing with his cigar.

"Yourselves."

"That's not what I mean. First impression, don't think."

"Hell."

"No. A paradox. It happened. If I forget, I can look at my number, or Sara's, or I can ask Sasha to open her mouth. But it happened the way a nightmare does, which is to say that it was real within a larger reality. So, a paradox. If you are forced to live in a nightmare, you survive by realizing that you can reimagine it, that some day you can return to reality. There is a poem by an American, I forget his name. He writes of 'The magnificent cause of being, The imagination, The one reality in this imagined world.' Esperanza is daylight to that night, the proof of the nightmare and our imagination."

At this point Carlos remembered Cecilia's picture on his desk.

"And the birds?"

"When you live as we did you look for signs, just as you do. When we first arrived at Auschwitz there were birds. I didn't know what kind, just brown birds, like the finches. They came for about a week and then the Nazis electrified the fences. I was out early the first morning they had the power on. A whole flight of these little birds came in and as they settled on the wire they made quick bright bursts of flame and smoke. The others did not know what was happening and they kept coming in and getting incinerated. The next day the birds did not come close to the camp. We saw them in the distance for a few days, but they never came close. At first I thought they had just naturally learned a lesson, but then I realized they had become sensitive to evil. From that moment on they became part of the reality we both imagined. Years later, when we docked in Buenos Aires, the last thing we did before setting out in our truck for this place was to buy some parrots and macaws from a stall in La Boca. These birds are their descendants, and ours . . . Sometimes I look at my friends here and I can see right into them and see the souls they carry of those who did not come out of the camps. I see their faces, hear their voices, and I remember. At such times I know they are with us, and for an instant I have saved my friends. It must be like what you experience in your stories. We are different, of course. My seeking is over, yours is happening. I hope you find Cecilia, my friend, but you cannot force these things. She is only part of what you are doing. You may find a way to keep her alive, but your way of life is in the stories, do you see what I mean?"

It had grown dark some time before Amos finished, and now Carlos listened to the night birds calling from invisible trees. He wanted Amos to continue, wanted more from the old man who lighted a cigar whose end glowed like a pinpoint of red light in the silence. For a moment Carlos thought he was tired, but then he realized that the silence was for him, that Amos was giving him the silence at the end of that long night so that he might absorb and take with him the idea that had kept Amos and Sara from being the people in the pictures taken by the Russian sergeant. When he understood he knew it was more valuable than any further words from Amos.

"Thank you," he said.

"Tell your stories," Amos answered, and with that injunction Carlos rose and went to his room, feeling for the first time since he'd seen Raimundo Garcia open his eyes that someone else truly knew what he'd seen and believed in it without a moment's hesitation.

After a quiet breakfast early the next morning Carlos bade the Sternbergs good-bye. He was about to get into his car when Sara stepped forward and took his face in her hands.

"Everything will come in its own time. Your gift will guide you."

As he drove off they were standing on the veranda, their birds flying around them, spiraling down from the trees.

The rush of wind through the windows carried the dry scent of wheat, and soon the wheat and thistle bushes became a great inland sea and Carlos drove into its glare eagerly. Once he saw a horse wading belly-deep in the mirage. In the distance black daws rose slowly, specks at first, then wings and bodies emerging as if the birds were freeing themselves from a magnetic field while in their wake drops of water remained in the air, like memory. It was then that he thought he saw Cecilia near a eucalyptus grove. He pulled off the highway and called her name as he broke into a run over the dried earth only to see her transformed into a fence post on which an owl sat with spread wings. He frightened it into the air where the *pampero* held it motionless as the owl looked down at Carlos before giving itself to the wind, pivoting on its right wing and rising over the pampas. He called Cecilia's name once again and the wind took it away with the bird, already grown small in the cloudless sky.

# 11.

When he told me about finding Cecilia in the mirage I almost wept. Terrible as it was to see her vanish once again before his eyes, he responded altogether differently from the way he had to her aborted escape from the warehouse. In place of despair he now felt only a problem of energy, of insufficient intensity of vision. Any doubts about her being alive had been erased by the Sternbergs, and I felt the same. Until then I'd hung back because of fear, but as Carlos recounted Amos' story the last resistance broke inside me, and when he repeated Amos' injunction to tell his stories I was finally caught up in a world where anything seemed possible.

On the following Thursday Carlos marched with the mothers in the Plaza de Mayo. Another man had joined them, and the sign he carried with a picture.of a young woman floated, sad and unreal, in the heavy summer air. Because of the heat they moved more slowly than usual, and that gave Carlos plenty of time to look at the Casa Rosada. As the circle went through its arc and Carlos faced the building he held his picture of Cecilia a little to one side so that he could see the windows of Guzman's office, Guzman, who by then everyone knew was the man responsible for the disappearances. Once Carlos thought the sun had reflected in the disks of someone's spectacles looking down on the procession, but it was impossible to be certain.

After the demonstration was over the mothers went off in small groups to each other's houses for food and talk and consolation. Carlos was about to leave too when he noticed that the man who'd joined them that day had taken refuge from the sun in the shade of a jacaranda on the far side of the plaza. He appeared tired and despondent and so Carlos went over and introduced himself to the handsome young man with blond hair and startlingly blue eyes.

His name was Gustavo Santos and he told Carlos that his sister, Marta, had been taken and he did not know if he could live without her. Carlos said later that the hatred in the young man, his rage at the generals, was so strong that he was afraid Gustavo might do something foolish. He had said he was ready to attack any soldier he saw even if it meant he'd be torn apart by machine-gun fire. Carlos tried to calm him, told him to take strength from the mothers, from himself. He invited him to his garden and Gustavo said he had wanted to come for a long time but he had been afraid. "Gustavo," he said, "you can never believe in them. Look at the building, think about the predictable mind hidden behind those pink stones. The mind of the Casa Rosada is no more alive, no more real, than you allow it to be. We are what is real, you and I, the mothers. We are so real that the men who may even now be looking down on us and making jokes about the Crazy Ones are afraid. Think of that! They disdain us publicly, have their toadies call us crazy in their papers, but they are afraid of a bunch of women and two men who have the courage to hold signs and walk in the heat of the midday sun. Hold on to that, Gustavo, believe in it."

It was not long after their conversation that the mothers decided they needed to increase the pressure on the generals, and the only way to do it was by calling greater attention to themselves. They spent several weeks deciding on the nature of their protest. Carlos met with a group which included Gustavo Santos as well as two French nuns who had felt compelled to join the cause to protest the silence of the Church. Alice Domon and Leonie Duquet urged strong action, and they all agreed to put their notions to the whole group, which would meet publicly in the Church of the Holy Cross. There they would draw up a list of demands and then march to the Casa Rosada in the middle of the day to present them to the generals.

At noon on a sweltering Thursday the mothers of the Plaza de Mayo assembled in the center of the city and began their procession toward the church. Half a dozen Falcons followed and Carlos noticed a number of intelligence people who tried to disguise themselves as sympathetic students or workers. Pedestrians moved into the shade of awnings to let them pass, and shopkeepers came out to watch. The owner of a jewelry store made an obscene gesture and spat in the face of a woman laboring to move her overweight body through the street. "Good riddance to the little fascists you all brought up! They deserve what they've got. Go home and leave us alone!" Carlos was so enraged that he was on the verge of attacking the man when Gustavo Santos put his hand on Carlos' shoulder and told him to let it go.

The march covered two miles of the city's most heavily trafficked streets and the Falcons followed close behind, ignoring streetlights and the white pedestrian triangles at intersections, following always at the same distance like pale green vultures, peregrine hawks, meat eaters. Sometimes Carlos caught the eye of the drivers, who returned his gaze blankly, contemptuously.

The Falcons frightened the people who had come out to watch, and by the time the marchers reached the church, whose double spires rose very clean and pure in the heavy air, the mothers had become invisible, fear having placed a milky white caul upon the spectators' eyes. Carlos went up the stairs past two men lounging near the ornate light fixtures, and by the time he entered the cool darkness of the church he knew something was going to happen.

They knelt, crossed themselves, gathered in the front pews where they waited silently for the priest, Father Ullmann, to give his blessing. Father Ullmann, a huge man whose girth made his cassock bulge like a wine barrel, assured them that God was on their side and faith would bring them through these unfortunate times. "The Church," he said, "is a visible sign of truth and strength. You can rely on it, and on those of us who serve, whenever aid and comfort are required." Alice and Leonie repeated Father Ullmann's injunction, adding that no one should abandon hope.

Then Maria Deleón got up and held the picture of her three children high above her head so that everyone could see. She reminded the mothers that once they had been too weak to do anything but carry pictures. Now they were growing stronger week by week, men like Carlos and Gustavo had joined, and there were promises from a dozen other men and teenaged boys that they, too, would begin to march. "I want my children," she said. "Together we can demand the return of all our people." She said there had been enough discussion, that the time had come to present their demands to the generals.

Hannah Masson carried her picture to the aisle where she turned and faced the group, her flame-red hair sticking out from under her scarf. She argued that their demands must be winnowed to a few clear statements of outrage that could not be ignored. "First we must force them to account for every single person known to be missing. Then we demand a timetable for their return, insisting that they tell us where our loved ones are being held. There must be visiting privileges and they must allow us to deliver food and clothing. This is no more than any civilized society would provide, even for its criminals!"

Hannah spoke so passionately that after she returned to her seat no one moved. She seemed to have exhausted all their energy, but then Gustavo Santos, who had been sitting with Carlos near the back, rose and slowly made his way to the transept. When he turned tears were streaming down his cheeks and his voice trembled so much that his first sentences were lost. He paused to get a grip on himself and wipe away the tears. Carlos told me his eyes were fierce as a jaguar's.

"Everyone," Gustavo said, "everyone here today has lost a son or daughter, a wife or husband. When Alice and Leonie speak, when Maria and Hannah tell us what must be done, it is as if they have taken words out of my own heart. If I were to speak about my sister, Marta, I would only be repeating what all of you have said at one time or another to each other, or to Carlos. I stand here

85

only to thank you for allowing me to grieve with you and, after today, to hope with you. I was not a man of courage before coming to the Plaza de Mayo. I am now. You have given me courage and hope, and more than either of those things, a way to see into the future which will not be like today, when some, perhaps all of us will have our people back. I want you to know that, I want you to know that I will go where you go, that I feel our strength."

After Gustavo spoke everyone agreed on the four things they must demand. A feeling of power was palpable as Father Ullman prayed and they moved up the aisle toward the great carved doors.

Seconds later Carlos heard the first shouts. A reverberation passed along the line of women reminding him of wind whipping through a field of wheat. Then everyone was running and by the time he reached the doors it was all over.

The security men had taken nine of the women, including Alice and Leonie, in their green Falcons. The mothers were in disarray—outraged, frightened, confused. Carlos did not know what to do. Some demanded that the papers be made to report the incident, others wanted to continue on to the Casa Rosada to present their demands. As they tried to find some order a Falcon cruised slowly up the street. None of the men inside looked at the mothers or Carlos. They merely stared straight ahead, affecting boredom. The talk died down and for a minute or two there were looks of absolute terror, whispered prayers. And then, as if the silent men in the Falcon orchestrated it, the mothers wandered off.

Carlos went home in a cab, explained what had happened to Teresa, and retired to his study, where he collapsed into his green velvet chair exhausted, dispirited, and confused. The kidnappings represented the generals' contempt, but they also signaled that the mothers had been infiltrated. He did not know which was more terrible—the disappearances, or the knowledge that one of the women was an informant.

That night Carlos dreamed of marching with the mothers around the obelisk. Soon the plaza filled with laughter from the Casa Rosada, and when he looked toward its pink facade he saw Cecilia standing between two men on the roof. One of them, the driver of the Falcon at the church, pushed her and she fell like a stone, shattering on the steps. It was then that he realized the other man was Gustavo Santos. He woke to another breaking sound. Shouting as he threw back the covers, he ran into the living room, half-expecting to find Cecilia, but when he turned on the lights he saw only glittering shards of glass and a blood-smeared brick in the middle of the carpet. Teresa came out of the hallway and they looked at each other for a long time across the broken glass. It was several minutes before Carlos remembered that his dream had given him the traitor.

# 12.

A week later Carlos and I sat quietly in his study while outside people slowly filled the garden. With the windows open we could feel the warm wind, the tail of a *pampero* come up from the south which stirred Carlos' memory of the pampas. He said that he saw the owl again, and its eyes were not hostile. Then Cecilia was rising with the bird, away from harm, and as he described her flight I heard his gift gathering strength, his imagination becoming full and powerful. Finally he nodded to me, indicating that he was ready, and we went out to the garden where the mothers' voices were somehow ordered into bravery, into belief that Carlos could undo what had happened at the church. He listened to their despair and rage, waiting, as he always did, for the word or image that would link the speaker's pain to his imagination. As soon as Gustavo Santos began to speak a change came into Carlos' eyes, a flicker of recognition, and then I knew this was what he had been waiting for and I felt my old bones tense in anticipation of what was coming.

"My sister, Marta," Gustavo began, speaking so softly at first that Carlos had to lean forward and cup a hand behind his ear to catch the words.

88

"My sister, Marta, was secretary to General Guzman. One day she saw something in his notes too frightening to talk about, even to me. She had gone into his office with letters for him to sign and when she put them down she saw the notes on his desk. He came in just then, and when he saw where she was he yelled and slapped her and demanded to know what she was doing. Before she could answer he fired her and ran her out of the office. She promised to explain what she'd seen the next day at lunch. When she did not appear I went to her apartment. It looked like a whirlwind had blown through the place. I knew it was because of Guzman. Do something, señor, give me my sister back!"

Gustavo's voice was like those intense images in a mirage which suddenly shiver and vanish. Each word came to Carlos with the tremulous unreality of an echo, and as he listened his eyes seemed to harden in the lamplight. As Gustavo spoke Carlos looked around the garden and saw how deeply moved the people were by the young man's pain, how they settled themselves in preparation for what Carlos would say about Marta's fate. Later that night he told me that when his gaze returned to Gustavo he was able to see behind his eyes and what lay there had never before appeared in his garden.

When Gustavo finished Carlos looked up to the lanterns and continued to stare at their wavering light for so long that his silence began to worry the people. Even Teresa, who was accustomed to such pauses, appeared concerned and she began to rise from her chair when Carlos gestured for her to stay where she was. He turned to Gustavo then and saw in his face the green Falcon moving off down Calle Cordova, Cecilia searching for him out of the rear window. He knew that if he exposed Gustavo the people might become violent, but if he remained silent, or asked for another person's story, he would lose the advantage his knowledge had given him. And so Carlos decided to explore the darkness. Perhaps the contempt he sensed deep inside Gustavo Santos could be turned against him, perhaps this impostor would find a justice he did not expect.

As he began Marta's story, Carlos felt the weight of his lies sinking into the clear water of the people's faith. His words were as duplicitous as the prayers of a priest who no longer believes, but says Mass and admonishes his flock in the fear that his apostasy is an aberration. The people were disposed to believe, aware that no one else in Buenos Aires could deflect the path of bullets, alter the charge of electricity, prevent the gang rapes. He was aware of all of this as he lied.

"I cannot see Marta very clearly. There is a white room and a bed, where she has waited now for hours. Sometimes she hears sounds from the other rooms, footsteps of guards in the hall. Earlier she had been with two women her own age. One had been beaten in her home, the other raped in the back seat of the Falcon that took her to the white room. Neither knew why she had been taken. They had never spoken against the generals, though the father of one and the husband of the other were sympathetic to the communists. That is the great pity for your sister, Gustavo. The generals are so afraid, so terrified, that the innocent suffer as terribly as those who oppose what is happening to our country.

"No, Marta is not very clear to me, but General Guzman is like a powerful flood of light into a sleeper's darkened room.

"I know, for example, that he was a little frightened when he found your sister reading those notes on his desk. Guzman is a fierce man who believes with all his heart that his fatherland is endangered, and the notion that someone close to him might try to harm it fills him with rage as well as grief.

"General Guzman comes from a long line of soldiers who have served Argentina, and in that legacy he sees something hallowed and more important than his life. Asked where his identity lies, he would tell us that it is in sacred duty. He conceives of himself as a patriot who believes that Argentines are a little mad, ungovernable by ordinary means, and capable of thriving again, of realizing our potential only if we accept the strong hand of people like himself. It is a religion to him, this belief, and even those who hate him know that he imagines a mystical Argentina where everyone believes exactly as he does. In this Argentina one could go from the north all the way south to Tierra del Fuego without meeting a man, woman, or child who would want to change anything, who would question the imagination of the generals.

"General Guzman is a student of history, and if we could enter his library in the elegant house where he lives happily with his family we would find an array of books devoted to the past as well as to the art of war. Sometimes he sits for upwards of an hour scanning the spines of his books, his eyes playing softly across the shelves and stopping long enough to allow him to recall what he knows. He is an expert in Roman history, having taught himself Latin in order to feel closer to the mind of the legionnaires who spread across Europe almost effortlessly implanting their will on people who had never heard of Rome and could not understand the ferocity which descended like a comet, a shower of swords and spears, while they were sleeping, or bathing, or even making love. General Guzman sees history from the time of the Romans to the rise of Hitler as a dark age in which men and women of many nations became philosophically perverted, denying the necessity of a single-minded vision, of the purity he believes Hitler saw and embraced as fiercely as a wild-eyed prophet did the words of his God on a windy mountaintop. And what he remembers most vividly in his library on these occasions is the betrayal of the Reich by socialists, democrats, communists, free-thinkers of all stripes who were so stupid that they could not understand that the vision of the millennium was worth any means necessary to attain it. That stupidity is a constant trial to him, like a piece of steel lodged near his heart, and whenever he thinks about it he is taken to the very edge of despair.

"And he thinks about it often. With others in the Army he has met secretly in heavily guarded houses deep in the jungle, or in cafés in tiny villages where he has looked across the table at Mengele and lesser exponents of that dream which he feels more than ever was defiled by the faint of heart, the women in man's spirit. With his colleagues he has long ago forgiven the atrocities as exaggerations, the Jews who went up in smoke a lie. When the Germans have had enough to drink they sing the old patriotic songs and he joins in, for he knows the songs and loves them. From time to time the feeling arising from this companionship is so strong that he sheds a tear and sometimes sees it mirrored in those of the men across the table. And when it is time for Mengele and the lesser lights to return to their anonymity, to the other names they have taken, he watches them leave the house like apostles whose suffering equals that of the early Christian saints. He watches them enter the jungle, disappear into the greenness, and he blesses them in their going.

"Yes, Gustavo, I see the man who sent your sister away much more clearly than I see her. Usually it is just the opposite. The disappeareds are very insistent in my imagination, very clear, while the soldiers, the guards, the secret police all have one face, the same eyes, move to the beat of the same heart. I think that is because the dream of power, the narrowness of their souls, leaves no room for the person, the individual. The cause overtakes the man as easily as a hawk swoops out of the sky and takes the foolish sparrow in its talons. It takes him away from himself, out of his conscience. That vacancy interests me, Gustavo, for it has always seemed to me that it is the birthplace, the womb of zealotry. Don't you agree?"

Gustavo's expression had not changed since the story began. He looked as dejected as a man standing on a cliff overlooking a rocky coast; despair in profile. Carlos studied the young man's face as he waited for a response. Suddenly it seemed familiar and in an instant he remembered a boy who had come to the Children's Theater just after he had taken over as chief playwright and dramaturge. The boy had been very gifted, a natural, but he left only a month or two later. Carlos was not sure they were the same. He did not want that to be the case. There was something obscene in the prospect of his having taught Gustavo to enter a persona so completely that he lost his individuality. For a moment Carlos wanted to claim illness, stand suddenly with his hand to his brow, anything that would allow him to return to his study where he could pursue the ghost of Gustavo Santos alone. Of course it was out of the question. He and Gustavo had to stay in the garden weaving and unraveling truth and lie in the jasmine-scented air.

Gustavo wavered first. His left hand rose and brushed his hair across his forehead. It was a remarkable gesture, for even such an automatic response expressed sorrow for his sister. But that was what the rest of us saw. For Carlos, Gustavo's talent had deserted him.

"I do, señor," Gustavo said, answering the question Carlos had asked. "It is a terrible, consuming dream they have."

"So we understand each other."

Gustavo was cleverer than Carlos thought. He was almost certain by this time that Gustavo knew what he knew. What disturbed Carlos was the difficulty of trying to make Gustavo understand what drove the men who paid him. It was useless to play Socrates to a dead Phaedrus. The only thing to do was to expose him, but it had to be done instructively. He had to allow Gustavo to participate in his own unmasking.

"I see Marta a little better now. She is small, is she not? and has a wisp of blond hair at her left temple which is very beautiful. If we are thinking of the same girl she could easily be picked up with one hand by a man of average size. How amazing, then, that she and others no larger can frighten all those men in uniforms. Is it not paradoxical, Gustavo Santos, that these men who claim to worship law, who claim to have devoted their lives to law, their souls to its restoration, devour little, lightweight girls like your sister Marta? Is it possible, Gustavo, that your sister and all the other girls who weigh so little that they might well float away on a moderate wind have consciously been chosen by General Guzman to fuel his desire? That he wants to burn everyone? But perhaps that is too difficult a question for us to address tonight, too close to metaphysics. Besides, I have wandered in my speculation. We were to have concentrated on Marta. Well, let us concentrate. I see her clearly. She has your eyes, coloring. If I am not mistaken she even has your voice, it is pitched only slightly higher than your own.

"I hear it clearly as she speaks to the other girls in her cell, which has been wired with a listening device. When Marta cried after one of the girls told her about what happens to babies born to mothers in captivity, how they are stolen and sometimes sold, the men listening in a distant room looked pleased. They congratulated themselves. It was terror they heard in her voice, and that was how they knew it was the right time to begin interrogation.

"Marta was taken to a dark room where she could not see the men standing behind a desk where a lamp had been turned into her face. As soon as she was forced into the chair her hands were tied behind her and the pain from the tight ropes was excruciating until her hands went numb. Someone behind the lamp began asking questions, asserting that she was a spy, that everyone knew it, that she had cynically taken the position in Guzman's office with

93

the intention of subverting the state. He says that a spy is a filthy thing, a living lie. How can she deny what she is? How can she live as she does? When Marta shook her head and said she was none of these things she felt hands on her breasts, hands which reached inside her brassiere, and then there was intense pain as her nipples were crushed. When she did not change her story wires were hooked to her and then she was jolted from her chair by the charge of electricity. The shock made her forget the pain in her nipples. The shock was regularly administered until she went into convulsions and lost consciousness.

"The next day, hardly aware of where she was, Marta was returned to the darkened room. Suddenly all of the lights were turned on, apparently so that she could watch as the men hooked the wires to her body. One showed her where the switch was located that would soon be tripped, allowing the electricity to burn into her once again. The questions come again and, since she is innocent, ignorant, unimaginative enough so that she cannot even make up plausible lies, the switch is flipped, the pain comes again. It went on like this for two more days until she could no longer stand it."

Carlos paused and sipped his tea. As he drank, his eyes played over the faces in the garden. Later he said we looked like all the other groups which had gathered there, eyes and bodies anticipating the reprieve, the miraculous escape, the defeat of the generals' imagination. Gustavo was rapt, wide-eyed, and he blinked when Carlos put his glass down, smiled sympathetically.

"As she waited for the next shock, the increased voltage, Marta went through an amazing transformation. The men in the room, those of you here tonight, Gustavo, Martín, even I know that Marta was on the verge of dying or going mad. Think about it. How many others had reached the same point in the basement of the Naval Mechanics School, the villa on the outskirts of the city, the old, crumbling police stations in the provinces? Dozens? Hundreds? We can only guess. But this time, unlike any of the others, something else happened. Look at the room in your mind's eye. Can you see the single lamp, the high-intensity bulb aimed into Marta's eyes? Can you see at the edge of the light, the corona, the vague, dark outline of a man in uniform? The glitter, perhaps of a

94

buckle, an insignia on the hat? Try to imagine the face of this dutiful soldier and the faces of his companions as they suddenly saw Marta begin to come apart, dematerialize, fragment. Can you see it happening? Her skin leaves her body, but instead of revealing muscles, organs, bones, the men in the room and those of us here in the garden see an elegant room, perhaps an apartment high above the turmoil of daily life, or the library in an elegant house in a fashionable suburb, the retreat of a high-ranking, important officer. We can see, Marta's captors and all of us here tonight, four men in uniforms sipping drinks, laughing, joking. One of them, a man of about fifty, with a shock of gray hair set off by darkly tinted glasses that all but obscure his eyes, says that it is time they investigate this man at the Children's Theater, the husband of that meddlesome journalist, this Carlos Rueda. There is some talk in the room that Rueda has vigorously preached sedition to his children, that he does so at secret meetings in his home. Ah, but wait a moment. There is another person in the room, a young man who has sat quietly, dutifully, even reverently in the corner, grateful for his drink and the enormous prestige conferred upon him by these presences. The soldier who has been talking turns to the young man, to Gustavo Santos, and tells him that he should prepare to attend one of Rueda's "séances" in the garden of the house on Calle Cordova. He will take a small cassette recorder and return with a tape of Rueda's seditious remarks. Since this Rueda is in the public eye because of his connection to the Children's Theater, they want firm ground to stand on, firmer, at any rate, than that necessary to kidnap and kill many others. What is important is getting evidence against this thorn in our side, this Rueda who thinks his magic will harm our cause. It is then that very specific plans are made for Gustavo Santos to infiltrate the mothers of the Plaza de Mayo, to pose as a fellow-sufferer, brother of a nonexistent woman who disappeared."

As he spoke, Gustavo's face, which had been the very picture of grief, looked strange. He was caught between disbelief that Carlos had discovered him, and panic over how he would escape. At the moment Carlos gave away the game the people stirred. There were gasps and whispers at Gustavo's name. Several people had gotten up and a burly man about Gustavo's age was trying to get to him. He had reached into his pocket when Carlos intervened. "Let him go. He is only a tiny part of what we have to fight. I want them to know we are not so naïve, that we can think like they do."

The man who had come after Gustavo reluctantly went back to his seat. Gustavo, who had risen when he thought he might be attacked, remained on his feet. He watched the man until he sat down again and then turned to face Carlos. It was remarkable. His face, which just for a moment as Carlos finished his story showed his contempt, his superiority, now looked like a fresco of grief.

"Señor," Gustavo said in a low voice touched with hurt, disbelief, with the amazingly pure sound of injured dignity. Gustavo let the word hang in the air for ten seconds, as if the effort to say what was on his mind was too much. He gestured with his left hand to the people.

"I thought you were supposed to help us. We are victims. How can you say such things about me? I hate Guzman, all of them, as much as anyone here. How could you think I am with them?"

It was then that Carlos sensed the danger to his reputation and the veracity of all he had done. Already in the silence following Gustavo's speech people were looking at him with disbelief. Questions about Carlos hung in the air like summer clouds. The actor in Gustavo had seduced them, his comments about his sister sounding like extensions of their own griefs. Carlos knew it was a critical time. Ironically he thought of it in terms of acting, feeling as if he had just come on stage and couldn't remember his first line. In the theater he might get away with the lacunae with any number of tricks, but not in his garden, not when the stakes were so high.

"I will let the people decide, Gustavo. If you are one of us, if I have lied, surely you will not object to emptying your pockets."

"Not at all," Gustavo smiled. "I was going to suggest it myself."

With that Gustavo took off his coat and turned out the pockets with an attitude of gentle sadness. He turned out his trouser pockets, slowly, deliberately, every movement protesting his innocence.

96

"Nothing," Gustavo said. "Look for yourself. A wallet, keys, some change."

"Your shirt," Carlos said.

Gustavo drew himself up in injured dignity. It was amazing, perfect. Even I began to think that perhaps Carlos' imagination had misfired.

"Absurd, señor. There is no reason for me to disrobe. You should apologize."

"Your shirt, then my apology."

A woman sitting next to me stood up.

"Go on," she said; "it won't hurt if you have nothing to hide."

Gustavo did not take his eyes off Carlos. Perhaps he could have pulled it off if he had not ignored my neighbor.

"No," he said, looking at Carlos, "I will not submit to such indignity."

Gustavo turned then, gracefully, beautifully, and reached for his coat, which he had placed over the back of his chair. He had not taken his eyes off Carlos, but he did when the woman put her hand firmly on his coat.

"Show us," she said.

Gustavo's eyes flickered and there was a momentary change from the carefully expressed pain to real anger before they gleamed again with injured pride. He was merely humiliated, and made stubborn by it. Anyone would understand.

"No."

"Then let me," she said. "Do you think an old woman will hurt you?"

As she reached for the top button of his shirt Gustavo stepped back, but two men had come up from behind so there was no place for him to go. He reached up and held the old woman's hands together in his own. What he felt, the exposure he could not avoid, was apparent in the thrust of his head, the way he had carried his hands to stop the old woman, the attitude of his body. The people talked among themselves, whispered, but that stopped when Carlos spoke.

"So we know. Let him leave. Gustavo Santos, or whatever his name is, is no more important than a single bullet, one blow of a club, one kick. Harming him will change nothing. It is what he thinks, what the men he believes in think, that we must deal with here."

Then Carlos turned to Gustavo and looked at him in a way I can only describe as gentle.

"Take your recording to Guzman and tell him that all we want is peace. All we want is for you to stop, to give us back our people. Think, Gustavo Santos, or whoever you are. What I said about your imaginary sister Marta has been true of hundreds of young women. Your generals are taking people who are ignorant of anything having to do with your power, your purges. Think about what it means for you to let it happen, Gustavo Santos. Can anything be worth that?"

As Carlos spoke I was reminded of the way boys bounce soccer balls against walls. He and Gustavo were looking at each other, but each word Carlos spoke caromed off Gustavo's eyes, which had grown harder and more contemptuous. Gustavo put on his coat. Then he turned and without saying anything walked up the flagstone path through the garden to the gate, which made a dry metallic sound as it slammed behind him.

We were all together again, united. As Carlos looked at us he understood that a change had taken place in his relation, in our relation, to the generals. It was no longer a guerilla war, a resistance by indirection. We were face to face now. The wires taped to Gustavo's chest acknowledged the existence of Carlos' garden and those who frequented it. The wires said Carlos and the rest of us had stepped over the line, strayed too far from Kilómetro Cero.

"There is one more thing before we go on," Carlos said. "This is perfectly logical. There are no regimes without spies. Think of Gustavo Santos, or whoever he is, as a floating eyeball, a disembodied ear. We must grant them the power of vision. Just think about the helicopters, the cameras, the tape recorders, the tapped telephones. They can penetrate every street, house, apartment, even this garden is not immune to their eyes and ears. They have penetrated the cafés and restaurants and melon shops, they have men like Gustavo on board ships in the harbor, and men like Gustavo have learned how to loiter in the dark corners of pool halls, dance halls. They want to make the city transparent, a city of glass. They can see everything they want to, but never forget that they cannot see beyond the distortion of their imagination where there is no color and everything exists in black and white. And that is why we will survive, because they do not have what is necessary to defeat us. The real war is between our imagination and theirs, what we can see and what they are blinded to. Do not despair. None of them can see far enough, and so long as we do not let them violate our imagination we will survive. Now, give me more names, tell me what has happened."

# 13.

After the humiliation in Carlos' garden there had to be some way for Gustavo Santos to salve his ego. Some people, unmasked as he had been, would take to drink, find the shards of the public self in a bottle, and continue more or less as they always did the next day. Others would brood, consider vengeance. Apparently Gustavo Santos was not like either of these types. The gentle, suffering brother of the fictional Marta must have been happy to shed his disguise and assume his own identity once again. He was, in reality, a captain in the Navy, Mario Rabán, affectionately called by his brother officers the "White Angel." It was a nickname not without irony. I can attest to that, as can Carlos, for not long after the phantom Gustavo left the garden and became his other self again he returned to his work among the intelligence people and cruised the city in his own Ford Falcon, cruised, as I have come to see it, like a bird of prey who plunged out of the darkness one night into a narrow street where many university students live in tiny apartments.

The story from this point is like all the stories Carlos heard or told: Mario Rabán and his companions had waited for a young woman for several hours, and when she turned into the street they abducted her. The tragedy doubled itself, as these things are likely to do, when her girlfriend, a seventeen-year-old by the name of Dagmar Hagelin, happened upon them. By this time Mario had taken refuge in a dark corner to watch the event unfold and we know it was he who shot Dagmar Hagelin in the back and then bundled her body, either wounded or dead, into the trunk of the Falcon, which then was seen by several people in different parts of the city on its way to the Naval Mechanics School. My theory, as soon as I heard about it, was that the event was linked to his humiliation that night in Carlos' garden. Perhaps Mario had killed other girls before Dagmar Hagelin made the mistake of trying to help her friend, but for reasons which I cannot begin to document I believe she was connected in his mind to Carlos and what had happened.

Carlos thought so too, except that for him the event had none of the distance, none of the objectivity I think informs my description. You see, he came to see me the next day, having heard about the shooting from certain people. He ordered a beer but did not touch it until the bubbles were almost gone. He looked terrible. "I shouldn't have let him go, Martín. Dagmar Hagelin is dead because I did not encourage the people to do what they wanted to." He softened as soon as I reminded him that he was not the type who could have let it happen, not even to someone like Rabán. He knew that everything would have come apart if Rabán had been harmed, that he would have descended to the gutter where the generals lived. The knowledge did not soothe his conscience. He grieved for the Swedish girl and it was that grief which brought everything into focus.

"They send this animal to spy on the mothers, let him kill children, a girl not much older than Teresa, and all I did was to send them a message, all I do is march with my sign, my picture of Cecilia. I think it is time to put our cards on the table."

It wasn't until a few days later that his comment made sense to me. To put it simply, he decided to have a talk with General Guzman.

Light rain misted the air the afternoon Carlos left the Children's Theater to call on Guzman. Although it was a two-mile walk to the Casa Rosada he decided against taking a cab. Wet streets, rain, the reflections of signs and store windows in the black mirror of the street always made him feel at home, in possession of the city. At such times he felt his own existence more intensely than during fair weather, as if the dry circle beneath his umbrella created an inviolable space, one inexplicably beyond the generals' threats. And Carlos thought it must be the same for everyone he saw as he made his way; even those people who caught his eye seemed, not far away, but deeply within themselves, strangely impregnable. Unless the generals chose to assign a cop to everyone walking in the wet streets of Buenos Aires they could not contain this simple but eloquent reminder of freedom. He said the idea held him for much of the distance between the theater and the Casa Rosada, that he thought of what it would mean if these little cones of freedom were to circle the ugly, squat building of the generals and expand, joining each other as the cells do in an embryo which must, by its nature, burst forth one day. It was a comforting, powerful thought, Argentina insisting on its natural time, breaking through the pink stones, the heavy doors, becoming itself.

While he thought of that freedom, of the stones developing cracks from the pressure of those little cones of power, not even the boarded windows of La Opinión dampened his spirits. The window against which Cecilia had placed her desk years ago gleamed as the rain turned its blackness into a clear reflection of the high rise across the street. He said a few words of encouragement to Cecilia, assured her that it would not be forever, that she must be patient and endure.

Five minutes later he was staring across the Plaza de Mayo at the Casa Rosada, missing Cecilia more than he had since she was taken. The dream of Argentina bursting out of that great stone facade seemed childish, and as for the encouragement he'd offered Cecilia, that was gone too, replaced by one of the few moments of doubt he'd had. He could not stay with the doubt, and to kill it he bore down on the building across the way, refusing to look any higher than the steps leading into its bowels.

In most countries here in the south, and by that I mean those governed by juntas, those in power do not exist. If they are seen it is from a great distance: a man with a killer's eyes gazing contemptuously from a balcony for a few minutes at a crowd below; a face behind the smoked windows of an expensive car; a carefully selected photograph in some lackey's newspaper. Their real haunts, the places where they do business, where they unbutton themselves, are hidden from view. But in Argentina during those years the generals believed so deeply in themselves that they left the doors of their sanctum open, inviting anyone who chose to do so to enter. Not many did, but the gesture was all important. To appear democratic, one of them said, is to be democratic. The lie glittered like a cheap shiny object bought on whim at a Sunday bazaar as Carlos entered the great hall and heard his footsteps echo from the polished marble floors to the portraits of our country's heros staring down at him from the rococo gilt walls. His footsteps joined those of soldiers moving with great self-importance across the length of the hall so that there was a cacophony of footsteps, of crisp military walking, of small explosions within the walls of the Casa Rosada which in turn could have been echos of real ones in the prisons outside, in fields miles away. Carlos walked through those sounds with only one thing in mind, one person who could even now be on the telephone ordering deaths, torture, unspeakable things. And then he walked out of the echo, having reached the base of the staircase where a young lieutenant watched him as contemptuously as if he had been some poor mad soul looking for food in trash cans.

Carlos knew the lieutenant was going to say that Guzman was not there, or was in a meeting, or out in the city on important business. That was how they finessed their openness, their false accessibility, reasoning that most people confronted with an official excuse would believe it, or be too discouraged to pursue the question.

"Please call anyway," Carlos said. "Tell him that Carlos Rueda has come to see him."

His name had no visible impact on the lieutenant, who grudgingly picked up the phone, dialed, and straightened in his chair. He mentioned Carlos' name and a moment later replaced the phone on its cradle.

"He is in, after all, but he has fifteen minutes, at best. Go up the stairs to the third floor, first door on the left."

There was another lieutenant in the anteroom of the general's office, a lean, dark man in his early twenties who looked efficient, capable. When Carlos sat down the lieutenant studied him with considerable interest, as if trying to understand why this nondescript, gentle man had been able to request an audience with his superior. Carlos looked at him, matching rudeness with rudeness until the man bent over some papers and began to write. Twenty minutes later a buzzer sounded on the intercom. His eyes were perfectly translucent when he looked up at Carlos and nodded in the direction of the polished oak door.

"Knock before you enter."

From the first time he had marched in the Plaza de Mayo, Carlos had wondered about the offices in the Casa Rosada, especially Guzman's. He suspected the walls would be covered with photographs of the general's career, group pictures of him at officers' training school, of the officers' messes in the divisions where he had served, treasured pictures with important men in the government. He imagined military insignia, the flags of divisions, but the moment he opened the oak door he was startled by how wrong he had been. The office was scarcely larger than the waiting room and the walls were bare, except for a picture of President Videla in a gilt frame on the wall behind the metal desk where Guzman sat, writing. The only concession to his rank and importance was a dark blue rug. Except for that the room was as pristine as a monk's cell, could have been such a cell with the simple addition of a cross on the wall in place of Videla, and Carlos said that first moment was truly a revelation, showed him, better than anything else, how single-minded his opposition was, dedicated, caught in the spirit of true believers everywhere. All the insignia, the regalia, the pomp of rank and service were inside, lodged in the depths of the pleasant-looking man, grown slightly bald but obviously in good physical shape, who made no sign to acknowledge his presence. Guzman's disdain was the only thing that Carlos found predictable in the office and he supposed it was merely a matter of style and thus was not angered by it. He said he thought it was comic relief, and almost laughed.

Carlos approached the desk and took a seat close to Guzman, who looked up then, smiled enigmatically, and the smile was the second surprise, for it softened the soldier, made him appear like any decent citizen one might meet in a café, at a bar, standing next to you at the Hipódromo for the races.

"Excuse me a moment," Guzman said, and returned to his writing.

Two large windows behind his desk gave onto the Plaza de Mayo. Carlos saw the top of the obelisk, the stretch of white stones where he and the mothers walked. Guzman could see everything by swiveling around in his chair and Carlos wondered how often the general had watched them, or if his disdain was so great that he lacked the curiosity to turn away from whatever business lay on his desk. At that moment Carlos found it hard to believe that Guzman would acknowledge the presence of the women in the plaza every Thursday. Guzman held himself aloof, preferring, Carlos thought, the endless sheets of data brought by subordinates, the strategies devised with other senior officers, to watching the slow, stately procession below his window. Guzman would no more do that than he would enter a dark street where the yellow explosion of a pistol momentarily illuminated the face of killers like Mario Rabán. The general was a theoretician who devised his plans in the pristine atmosphere of a monk's cell.

"Now, Señor Rueda, what do you wish to see me about?"

His voice was formal but relaxed, calculated, Carlos thought, to put him off balance, to make him feel that all the power in the room lived in the general's words. Carlos looked at him for a long time before speaking, telling him with his eyes that he was not afraid.

"My wife, the nuns, your white angel."

There was the faintest suggestion of a smile in the corner of Guzman's mouth as he sat back in his chair.

"You must remember this is not a children's theater, señor. In the adult world there is little patience for riddles."

"Tell me where my wife is."

Guzman passed his hand over his face, as if to say, "Oh yes, this tiresome business again." What he actually said was even less forthcoming.

"Forgive me. I do not understand. Your wife is missing?"

"You know she is."

"She has committed offenses?"

"She has been human."

Guzman's expression became a little more pronounced, giving away the emotion he was holding inside, some combination of anger and contempt. He pulled the cuff of his left sleeve tight, brushed a speck from the desk.

"What is her name? I have a list of subversives we have arrested for crimes against the government."

"It is not only her name, so long as you are looking. She is Cecilia Rueda. The nuns are Alice Domon and Leonie Duquet." Then he gave the names of the rest of the women who had been taken from the church. Guzman flipped through the pages of some documents.

"There is no record, señor. You have made a mistake."

Carlos had memorized that line, knew it exactly from the moment he decided to confront the general. It would have been miraculous if Guzman varied from it by a single word. He knew that the general and everyone else in the Casa Rosada would deny knowing anything, but that was not why he had come. He had come because he wanted a face to remember, and Guzman's was the best face, the one nearest the heart of the government. He also wanted Guzman to see him, close up, not frozen in the photos his agents brought him. The demand and the answer were merely the form in which such knowledge could be exchanged, Cecilia's name Alice's, Leonie's mere counters, really, at the beginning of a game that would last until either he or Guzman gave out, or was killed. Knowing all of this in advance Carlos had not even felt especially angry as he walked through the rain to the pink, cold building, but he had not anticipated the smoothness, and he was surprised when he realized that it was a strain to control himself, that he was actually measuring the possibility of doing something violent. Guzman sensed it, for his eyes changed, as if he were no longer looking at a harmless man who made his living pandering to the imaginative whims of children, but at someone capable of the extraordinary, a man who could reach into the pocket of his coat. Guzman tried, as casually as possible, to conceal the movement of his left hand beneath the desk as he pushed a button which brought the lieutenant in from outside. The door flew open with a bang.

"You might as well wait a moment, Hector. Señor Rueda is about to leave and I need to tell you some things."

Carlos smiled at Guzman. "My wife," he said, "the nuns."

"Their names are not on the list so they have not committed any crimes. If you do not know where they are it is because some leftist group has taken them to make us look bad. We do nothing to innocent people."

"I see. Well, then, since you will not tell me where my wife is, or what you have done with the women from the church, perhaps you might explain why you sent that double man, Gustavo-Mario, to spy on people whose only desire is to see their loved ones."

Guzman glanced at Hector.

"The meeting is in Castillo's office?"

"Yes."

"I am busy, señor, and have no time for your children's games."

"And I anticipated your business, general. I could not keep you from it, even if I tried. I would simply like to be able to understand why you do it. Is it sheer power? Messianism? Have you had a vision?"

"Enough riddles, señor. We are in power because we need to be in power. We will relinquish it when Argentina is safe again."

"One more riddle, General, a short one, whose answer is not far away. Why do those women march in the Plaza de Mayo?"

"Even animals have mothers, Rueda. I would not dispute that."

"They want their children back. None of us can still quite believe that a bus was stopped in La Plata and you took the children."

"I know nothing of children. We act against sedition. The women are welcome to inquire as to whether they have criminals on the lists."

"Is Cecilia on the list?"

"You are tiresome, Rueda. If your wife is not at home perhaps she has grown tired of you. I understand that happens often among artistic types."

And that was the end of it. The slur was perfectly timed, for Guzman rose as he spoke and prepared to leave for his meeting, real or imagined. Carlos felt as if he had been lost and turned into a blind alley where, at the end, he encountered Guzman's brick face. He knew that if he could somehow open Guzman's head, peer inside his skull, he would find a brick wall. He too got up and slipped on his coat.

"One day, General, you will remember this conversation, not for what I have said up to now, but for this: Your belief would reduce us in size, shrink us to the little heads the forest people used once for barter and symbols. They were primitive and so it is easy to understand their desires. You are not. You believe that cutting off our heads and then shrinking them will stop us, that the knowledge of your willingness to do it will frighten everyone. You believe you can kill us. That is what you will remember, that you made the terrible mistake of not knowing what to kill. The danger to you is invisible and perhaps you will never understand it."

"More riddles?"

"If you choose to only hear riddles. I will give you the name of this one. It is imagination."

The sky had opened by the time Carlos was on the street again. Water ran up to the edge of the sidewalks, poured in sheets from awnings, slowed traffic to a crawl. He said it was strange, being back out on the street, repulsed, denied, even defeated in a way by General Guzman. At the same time he felt secure in that little circle of privacy cast by his umbrella. He had gone into the Casa Rosada and come out, a feat no less harrowing, from a certain point of view, than Daniel's visit to the lion's den. No, it was considerably less than defeat. He had made his statement, and he had come away with Guzman's face—harsh, practiced, unforgiving, but in the end a human face, flawed by singleness of mind, zealotry, conviction. It was the face of the night, the one which had appeared to everyone who had been taken, a face no better or worse than those which had looked out from beneath the skull and crossbones of the SS, the faces of judges looking down upon some poor bastard on his way to Siberia, the faces of Afrikaners pushing out the infidels, making room for the chosen people. He could deal with that face, and so, he thought, could anyone who came to him.

As he went along the boulevard to the theater, safe, encased in the circle of identity which the umbrella magically gave him, he decided that all he could do was to increase the pressure, demand more from himself. Even then he felt as if he was holding back and that frightened him, for from the beginning he knew the only salvation for himself, for Cecilia and for all the others was in giving everything. It was later that night, on the way home from the theater in the old Peugeot, that he first thought about the play which would be called *The Names*.

Teresa was not home when he let himself in and left his coat and hat in the tiled entry. He was glad because he wanted some time alone to think about Guzman's face and how to show the people that it was only human. He wanted time, too, simply to be in the house and commune with Cecilia. He knew, without a doubt, that she was still alive, and as he sat there in his velvet chair she seemed to be forcing her reality on him with the same intensity he'd felt after leaving Esperanza. His proof was Guzman's face, for he knew that if they had killed her something would have shown in the general's eyes, in his gestures, even while he maintained that he had never heard of her.

# 14.

I missed the next three weeks at Carlos' house because of a bad case of flu. When he learned of my illness he came by every few days and added his concern to Eugenia's, who hovered over me like a mother hen with her soups and kind words. Teresa showed up unannounced one day after school and offered to read to me, or play cards, whatever I liked. My fever was so high that even the simplest game was beyond me, but I told her that if she wanted to she could read a little from Borges.

For half an hour that afternoon, while the weak sun lighted my bedroom, I listened to her lovely voice, a carbon copy of Cecilia's, bring to life that wonderful speculation, "The South." In a matter of minutes I was aware of a correspondence between the old man's skewed vision of reality and the world Carlos had begun to see. Always in Borges you are conscious of the "as if," the playful relationship between the world of his stories and the one we live in. Well, it struck me that Carlos simply leaped beyond anything Borges gave us, for the "as if" was erased whenever he went into his garden, replaced by what all of us who listened to him had come to believe was the literal truth of Carlos' imagination. As Teresa described Dahlmann going outside the café to confront his fate, her father seemed to be in an identical position: Remain inside and be miserable in what passes for reality, or open the door and enter that which would make itself known only as it was being created. That new way of thinking about Carlos was both frightening and energizing, for after she left I found my own imagination running wild as I envisioned Carlos going through a door, his only weapon language that welled up from deep within, and then outside, in a dark, murky terrain, the sound of a confrontation, of an unseen knife clashing against Carlos' words.

The next time I went to Carlos' house I told him about it. He laughed before I'd finished and put his arm around my shoulders, pulling me close.

"You're like all good friends, Martín. You flatter me even though what I do has no art. I am simply a place, a locus, where the stories occur. There is more art in one of Borges' sentences than in everything I have said in my garden."

I would have disputed the point if he hadn't made it clear that it was time for me to leave him alone. When he appeared twenty minutes later people began imploring him to help even before he settled into his chair. He listened carefully, responding when he could, and then Rubén Mendoza asked him if he could see his son and daughter-in-law and grandchild, and Carlos told their story.

He appeared so exhausted by the time he finished that I didn't think he'd go on, but then an old man in the front, old even compared with me, began to speak in a voice so soft that I could hardly make out his words. Carlos had to get up and kneel beside him, but evidently that made Solomon Levy angry. In any event, I was as surprised as Carlos when he said, "Do not demean yourself. I can speak loudly enough for you to hear."

Carlos went back to his chair and Solomon began speaking in a voice which Carlos later told me immediately took him out to the pampas, for his words were formed around an accent he recognized as soon as the old man explained where he'd come from.

"My home is in the south," he said, "and your friends, Amos and Sara, sent me. They say you have the power to make things happen again. Is that true?"

"It is sometimes, old man. Talk to me."

With that Solomon Levy half-turned in his chair so that the rest of us could hear his story.

"It was in 1942 and we were celebrating my grandson's bar mitzvah. Since the apartment was on the second floor at the back of the building and faced away from the street we felt safe in our own little world. All of us had scrimped and saved so that there was almost good food on the table due to the talent of my daughter in cooking. We had just begun eating when the Nazis broke in. There were screams, shouts, that was all we had against their strength and guns. A few days later we were put on trains. Everyone died but me. After the war I returned to the city and spent a year looking for Avrom because my daughter, just before she got into the boxcar, shouted that she hadn't seen him, that perhaps he'd gotten away. I looked for thirty years before coming to Argentina. I want him as much now as I did then. Can you see where he went? Did they kill him?"

Carlos saw the skeletons he had come to know as Amos and Sara, the rat running off with Sasha's still warm tongue. For several minutes he saw nothing else and then those images were superimposed on piles of bodies, on the cold foggy countryside of Germany, Poland, France. He did not know if he could go that far, and he said later that he was surprised when the words began to flow, the images coming as clear and fresh as if a picture had just developed.

"As soon as they burst into the room Avrom ran to help his mother, but just as he reached out for her one of the Nazis struck him with the butt of his rifle and sent him flying. Shouts and cries filled the room as he lay next to the sofa, his head on fire. He would remember for years that all he could see at that moment was the triangle of space between the back of the sofa and the wall, and that he crawled into it fully expecting to be shot or dragged out. Neither happened. As suddenly as the Nazis had come they were gone with his family. He wanted to leave his hiding place then, to go after them, but every time he moved the world spun around and all he could do was listen to the thunder of footsteps going down the stairs and then to the lorries' motors whining and the high pitch of the gears. It was very quiet for a minute, and then he heard a banging sound and thought one of the Nazis had come back for him. He was a little stronger and was able to look around the side of the sofa where he saw the door sagging on sprung hinges, flapping against the wall. That sound marked the end of his childhood, that and the roughness of the diesel motors which had preceded it.

"Avrom remained in his hiding place until it was dark. The pain stayed with him, as if it had been wrapped around his head, but he was no longer dizzy, and he realized that he had been hungry for a long time. Somehow it was worse in the dark, as if the whole squad of Nazis were there, simply waiting for him to come out, and when he did, when he stuck his head out from behind the sofa, he was almost certain they were waiting for him. Feeling his way to the table, his hand settled into the middle of the cake his mother had baked and he lifted the plate and took it back to his hiding place and ate until he was almost sick with sugar and fear. He slept after that until the wind out of the north began blowing in such a way as to swing the broken door on its one remaining hinge, making it squeak unbearably in the dark. Then he went to sleep again and when he woke he thought the sound had become much louder and it took some time for him to understand that it had been his own shout, or scream, that echoed in the room.

"What happened to Avrom during the remaining years of the war was not pleasant, yet he was by no means the only child suddenly left alone, and like the others who survived he grew strong almost overnight. Avrom knew he would die with the stale remains of his bar mitzvah cake if he did not leave his sanctuary behind the sofa, and so, late the next day, he began his life as a scavenger with two other boys he met, a life of eating garbage, stealing anything at any time that might help him survive, and always praying for forgiveness.

"By the end of the war Avrom had made his way to Paris where he worked as an apprentice to a silversmith, who paid him a few francs a day and sometimes threw in a stale loaf of bread. Despite his poverty, he was in perfect, even robust health, although he had lost his left eye in a fight with a boy outside Warsaw over the remains of a rabbit.

"When he had time, mostly on Sundays, Avrom frequented those quarters of Paris where Jews lived, always hoping that somehow someone in his family had survived. He was convinced his grandfather and parents had died in the camps, but he was also driven by a persistent dream, an obsession, about his sister. It was not until several years after the war ended that he no longer felt compelled to follow certain young women with long raven-colored hair and a special way of tossing it out of their eyes. Half a dozen times he could not contain himself and went up to the woman, took her arm, and said his sister's name just as the stranger turned and confronted him with an angry look, a sharp oath.

"By the time Avrom gave up his search for his sister he had become skilled as a silversmith and the man who had taught him offered to take him on as a partner. That was the first of the new things that began unfolding in his life, new growth to cover the old scars, soften the memories that could be softened. The second of these events occurred when he met, fell in love with, and married the daughter of an Argentine who had gone to live in Paris. Erica told him he was the first happy thing to happen since she watched her beloved Buenos Aires disappear over the horizon as the family followed her father's dream to live in the City of Light. It was good in many ways that they found each other, perhaps even more for Erica than Avrom, for six months after they married thieves broke into her parents' apartment and killed both her father and mother.

"Erica was inconsolable until the birth of their daughter, Isabel. By the time the little girl was three years old Avrom had amassed enough money to buy his own shop and with their new position and income the life of Paris opened up for them. Yet they both felt something was missing, although it was a long time before they could speak of such things to each other. Avrom knew without Erica having to tell him, for sometimes he came upon her unaware, sometimes when the baby was asleep next to her on the sofa, and awake or asleep he saw an expression she never revealed when she knew he was looking at her. Sometimes she saw him watching her and then she immediately tried to brighten up, force a smile. Finally he pressed her and she broke down. She had never wanted to leave Argentina, the only things that made life outside Buenos Aires bearable were Avrom and Isabel, but she had to admit that even they were no longer enough.

"That was some time ago, nine or ten years, I cannot be certain, but what is clear is that from the moment Erica spoke Avrom began to meditate on how he might change things. He looked up Argentines who were living in Paris and brought some of them into their lives. But that look of having been forced into the world of the refugee, a world in which Avrom himself had grown up, never completely left Erica's face, not even when their apartment was filled with South Americans. And then he realized that Erica's longing had mirrored his own, all along.

"Not long after that discovery they took the train for a holiday to Warsaw. Erica loved the old city, and was endlessly patient when Avrom was gone for hours to explore the old neighborhood. The family's apartment building had been torn down to make way for a commercial structure which seemed to him a terrible grave marker for what had happened there. He went to the street where his grandfather had lived, went to every house asking if anyone had seen the old man, and when they said no asked if they could remember the last time they had seen him. Even then the people shook their heads and it was with an image of such negativity that Avrom returned to Erica and Isabel. A day or two later they boarded the train for Paris.

"Avrom had come to the point where he admitted to himself that a large part of what he wanted would never be available, that the happiness he felt with Erica and Isabel would never be completed by the smells of remembered cooking in his family home, that none of his family would ever know his wife or child. That home and those people were only air and dust and he knew that a portion of his soul was withering because he longed, silently, but strongly, for air and dust. That was why he had turned to Erica soon after the train left Warsaw and told her that he wanted all of them to go home to Argentina.

"They sailed not long afterwards for their homeland and I can see the indescribable delight in Erica's eyes as the ship docked and the city took shape out of the flat land, the skyline of Erica's imagination. That night, at a hotel not far from La Boca, they made love to the distant sound of tangos, and it was in the echo of a tango that their son, Geraldo, was conceived.

"That is where it ends for me, old man, with your grandson and granddaughter coming home. I do not know where they are, but Avrom must be practicing his trade, and if you look you will find him."

After the people left and we talked a little about Avrom Levy, Carlos excused himself and went inside. It was still quite warm, and through the open doors I saw him take his guitar from the case whose red velvet lining shown like blood in the bright light. Sometimes when Cecilia was on his mind he played the Villa-Lobos "Prelude," and I knew as soon as its great, gliding glissandos floated out into the garden that he was listening for her in the music, which arched up again and again from the unutterable sadness of the ground bass where each variation began. When he finished he sat cradling the guitar, his arms wrapped around its gleaming rosewood form, totally absorbed in some inner vision I had no intention of intruding upon.

On the way home in the cab I asked the driver to go the long way round, down by the docks. Carlos' story about Avrom and Erica came to life again when I turned to watch the city, for it seemed to me that I was seeing it as Erica must have done that day, as a home she'd never left, and then I felt like a fool. Avrom and Erica's story, all those I'd heard over the last few months in Carlos' garden, had a common theme running through them which I'd missed as I searched for obscure connections, numinous meanings in his conjurings. The stories were bound together by the notion of breaking through and returning, and it was then that I realized how apt my feeling was when I'd imagined Carlos going through the door opened by Borges' character in "The South." Perhaps it was merely chance, but my recognition that night of the pattern in the return of the Levys, of Carlos and Dahlmann going through the door to confront the unknown, of Angela Mendoza being thrust through another door into the astonished arms of her grandfather, was a prelude to a new and startling development in Carlos' powers.

# 15.

The next day Carlos turned his attention to a new play for the Children's Theater, *The Names*. Someone who hadn't known him well might have thought that in taking his inspiration from the Sternbergs Carlos was retreating, finding a haven in the past and memory, rather than challenging the darkness beyond the door. I attest flatly, unequivocally, that the play, which was a heroic act as well as the harbinger of tragedy, took him light-years ahead, that the real but wondrous world he entered going up the poplar-shaded avenue months ago in the pampas, the world of birds with the names and perhaps the souls of human beings dear to the Sternbergs, was a tribute to the power of imagination which had survived events that should have killed it. In the swirling, fluttering cacophony of macaws and parrots and jungle birds of unknown species Carlos Rueda found a picture of how Argentina could survive, and, more personally, a logo for the gift that came his way that distant afternoon on the stage of the Children's Theater.

He never told me exactly what went through his mind. All I know is that he was unable to suppress the images of Esperanza's birds. He told Esme and Silvio that the work they were planning for the next few months, some original skits of his own, two of Esme's, a fanciful version of a Grimm's fairy tale, were sops to the generals' power, artistic acquiescence to the force behind Kilómetro Cero. If they continued with the normal fare the theater had been offering for the last ten years they were really little more than quislings who, in their silence, ignored their responsibility to the city's children. "They deserve to know what is at stake," he said, "and how they might combat it."

Silvio, the eternal cynic, the constant naysayer who believed in more things than his pride could ever let him admit to, told Carlos he thought the idea was suicidal.

"The theater survives so long as the generals believe we give the kids harmless tales about mythological characters, little histories of gauchos and goblins, fairy tales that the old bastards themselves fell asleep to. The second they even suspect political content they close us down. What do you propose to eat, the dust that will accumulate on the seats?"

"I agree with Carlos," Esme said. "We have to do something too."

And so, after much recrimination from Silvio, which Carlos and Esme knew was at least partially histrionic, it was agreed that Carlos would shelve for the time being the manuscripts of mythological plays he had been preparing and devote his time to *The Names*.

For the next week Carlos sequestered himself in his house, and then for two more weeks, until Silvio and Esme began to wonder if he would ever show up again. Much of the time was spent looking out at the garden from his study, investing it with the life and color of Esperanza. Carlos decided that he wanted to make a realistic play depicting the Sternbergs' and Shasha's stories, but for reasons he could not understand each page of *The Names* was more inert than the last. Every morning he rose early and tried to repair what had gone wrong the day before, but it was no good. When he gave the draft to Esme he spent a wretched hour alone in a little coffeehouse down the street from the theater until she came in and said, gently but firmly, that it was the worst thing he'd ever written.

When he decided to let the play go for a while he became

irritable, provoking quarrels with Silvio, saying things to Esme that hurt her, and then begging both of them to forgive him. He was no better at home. Teresa came to see me once, frustrated and in tears because she couldn't understand what was wrong with her father. As we drank cocoa and played a little Scrabble I tried to explain that something was in the process of getting itself born in his imagination. I'd seen him half a dozen times during this period at the Raphael. He said that every time he tried to work the images into ideas the whole conception came apart. And so, while I had a number of misgivings, I told Teresa not to worry, aware as I did so that I was very close to lying.

Fortunately everything came together for him a few days after Teresa's visit. He quickly finished a first draft, and a week later presented Esme with the second. Once again he went to the coffee-house, but instead of agonizing over her response he worked on the music for the play, a melody I can still hear, strangely lyrical but disturbing, like a combined love song and elegy. Esme was crying when she arrived, and Silvio, who'd come along, was also moved.

I didn't see much of Carlos for the next few weeks while he and Silvio worked on designing the set and costumes. When he finally called it was to invite me to take a look at what they'd achieved. I got there around noon, and as soon as I passed through the doors Carlos called for me to come up on the stage, his voice echoing in the empty theater along with the noise of the people busy building the set. Half a dozen skeletal structures were placed diagonally across the center of the stage. I had no idea what to make of them. Off to one side Carlos and Silvio were bent over a folding table studying designs on sheets of butcher paper. When I came up the steps Carlos leafed through several sheets before finding the one he wanted.

"The set," he said, "what do you think?"

The skeletal forms rising behind us would become gaunt metallic trees, but their stark feeling was balanced by child-birds sitting on perches which spiraled up from the base to the tops. I can't say that I entirely understood the effect. It reminded me at once of the colonial wrought-iron work one sees everywhere in Buenos Aires, of electrical pylons in the industrial areas, of prison bars.

The background showed a grove of ethereal eucalyptus fading away into the pampas, and their presence lessened the severity of the trees.

"Your vision of Esperanza?" I asked.

"Partly, but of something else too. Everything that's happened."

When I was leaving Carlos invited me to the rehearsals. He was always thoughtful in that way. While I'd accepted his invitations before, this time I declined. There was something a little mysterious, even magical in what he'd shown me that I thought might be diminished if I watched the whole thing being put together. That doesn't mean I forgot what I'd seen. Over the next few weeks the images frequently interrupted my own work, and as the date of the premiere grew closer I felt excited and, in a way I couldn't quite grasp, a little uneasy.

The premiere was set for two o'clock on a Saturday afternoon. People were already filing in when I arrived at one. Half an hour later the theater was full of children and adults, and late-comers were forced to line up three deep in the back. It was a noisy, happy crowd, but I couldn't shake the uneasiness that had edged my feeling about the play. I'd found a seat near the front on the left side, and as I watched the crowd I recognized two men a few rows back who were trying to look inconspicuous. I don't know how to describe them, but that isn't important. They were obviously security people—their awkwardness gave them away as surely as if they'd appeared in uniform. My impulse was to get up immediately and go backstage to warn Carlos. I didn't because I suddenly realized he knew they'd be there. Moreover, I understood they must have been on his mind all along and were as much a part of his intended audience as the children and their parents.

As I was wondering what to do with this revelation the lights dimmed to a faint reddish glow. A moment later the theater went dark and remained that way a long time before a melody of single notes filled the room, a plaintive, haunting sound played in the deepest register of the guitar. The music ceased suddenly, unexpectedly, as a pinpoint spotlight came on, illuminating Carlos sitting in a chair at the edge of the stage only a few meters away from me. He was dressed simply in a turtleneck sweater and corduroy

trousers. The last time I'd seen him he'd been excited, confident, but that was gone now. He bent forward, cradling the guitar in his arms, his left foot resting on the wooden stool. The neck of the glistening Ramirez guitar pointed like an arrow at the still invisible trees. What struck me was the intensity of his expression, the pain in his eyes. People who didn't know him would have put it down as acting, and they couldn't have been faulted for it. But it was the memory of Cecilia that gave birth to his intensity. She was as startlingly there as the shadow of an atomized person burned into the concrete abutment of a bridge at Hiroshima. It was an over-whelming connection and I was so caught up in it that I almost missed his first words because he spoke so softly. A faint yellow light now illuminated the stage behind him, revealing the line of trees as ghostly but perceptible presences.

"Look," he said, half-turning to the trees, "a metal forest, cold and denuded as Argentina, yet life remains among the leafless branches, voices, names.

"This is a play about memory and desire, about words and the sounds we live in. Think of it. Argentina tells us where we are. Names make us known to family and to strangers. La Plata makes the river ours, allows us to know it from all other rivers. Buenos Aires is the name of home. Calle Cordova, my street, is unlike any other because of its name. It is that way with your street, too. Names are the foundation of everything.

"Think of it. Names tell us about a life and the memory of that life. But in Argentina names are not like they are elsewhere. Here, now, they are as easily erased as markings on tissue paper. Now the page of Argentina is clean of names that belong there, that have a right to be there. So this is also a play about history, how that happened.

"Argentina is full of names. Our memories are full of names. Names are as natural as trees, birds, breathing. They are the right of a person, but there are those who believe they can take the people and their names away, and this must not happen. Names must never, never be stolen again.

"In the pampas, down a tree-lined lane, live three people who once saw the names of loved ones and strangers burned out of life, yet they keep those names alive in memory. They give the names

of those who vanished to birds so that the sky above their *estancia* is always alive with flying names.

"Names fly here too, at the Plaza de Mayo on signs held aloft by those who loved the people with those names.

"This is a play about what we must do to keep the names alive."

The lights came up then, a faint glow of yellow. As Carlos touched the strings the music was faint as an echo. Slowly the tremolo, played in the bass, filled the theater with a sound of longing and desire, and as the melody emerged a dozen children moved in stately procession onto the stage from both wings. They were costumed like birds with fantastic plumage. When they crossed to the center of the stage they turned and the other side of the costumes revealed huge, almond-shaped eyes which stared at us as the children circled the metal trees and the music ceased with a shuddering chord as the stage went dark.

A few bars of the melody sounded faintly before dozens of spotlights shown on the perches where the children had ascended. The lights grew stronger and the children swayed to the rhythm of Carlos' music, each child calling out names like questions:

"Maria Traven?"

"Ernesto Milinda?"

"Francesca de la Rosa?"

Dozens of names were called loudly, softly, and the children were singing. There was an amazing counterpoint between the guitar and the songs of the names. It was as sweet and haunting as anything I'd ever heard until suddenly, with no transition, the voices ceased and the guitar sounded a harsh, dissonant chord as a winged apparition, half-black, half-white, strode onto the stage, its huge wings tapering at the ends to large, grotesque hands. It moved quickly across the stage and climbed the nearest tree to a perch where it enclosed the child there in its wings. The light faded from the perch as the voice of the child became fainter and fainter until it was silent. Then it moved to another perch, and another, each time taking the child there by the throat. All along the line of trees children frantically called the names of those who had vanished. But it did no good. The apparition moved from perch to perch, enfolding children in its grasp. The melody by then had

gone deep into a minor key, and each time the apparition struck there was a shuddering, dissonant chord. And yet the calling of the names never ceased, not even when the stage went dark.

When the lights came up again the children who had disappeared returned to their perches, feathers torn and streaked with blood. The apparition ran from one tree to the next, but it could no longer climb to the perches. As it wandered back and forth, dazed and disoriented, a line of girls in simple black dresses, their heads covered with white scarves, moved across the back of the stage until they circled the apparition. One of its wings rose high above the girls, fluttered, and then went out of sight as the girls went off stage right. Then the lights came on stronger than before and the melody of Carlos' guitar rose to a major key. With the last chord the audience stood and cheered. Carnations sailed onto the stage and Carlos gathered them and gave them to the children.

There was a party afterward backstage. It was so packed with children I couldn't move. Everyone was excited, but it was too much for me. I looked around for Carlos and finally saw him coming toward me with his arms around Esme and Teresa. I was almost afraid of what I'd see when he got closer, but thankfully that amazing presence of Cecilia had faded from his eyes. He seemed relaxed, almost happy, as he asked me to have dinner with the three of them. I was tempted, but the idea of two long cab rides across the city was too much so I begged off, but not before telling Carlos about the men I'd seen. He laughed when I said they'd worried me.

"It would bother me if they hadn't come. I think they're just saying 'We're here.' "

That was one of the few occasions when Carlos was wrong.

Late that night Carlos went to bed tired and fulfilled. Almost as soon as he lay down he was dreaming of playing his guitar for the generals, who once again held Cecilia between them. He did things with the guitar he'd never been capable of, discovered tonalities never heard on the instrument, achieved dexterity with both hands which amazed him so much that he wondered if they were his hands at all. Then Cecilia was free and they were walking down a beautiful tree-lined street so full of each other that it seemed as if they had never been apart. He could not quite understand her words but it did not matter. Her voice was like music, like water splashing in the fountain of a tiny plaza where they went to be alone. Then the sound of the water rose to a scream. He sat up in the glare of the light in his bedroom and saw three men coming at him, saw the truncheon raised in the left hand of the man who had watched him that day at the Church of the Holy Cross. Teresa was screaming "No, no, no!" and then the pain of the blow made her voice sound out of phase, like a turntable that has lost its power. Carlos struggled to get up and felt another blow and then the room was red and white and Teresa's voice faded into darkness.

# 16.

The pain in his head was so intense he could not think. He did not even know who he was, or that he lay on the blood-soaked carpet in his bedroom. His whole existence was concentrated in his head, while his body was no more substantial than the chalk outlines of a torso in a bad detective film. He imagined the huge tires of a Number Four bus flattening as they crushed his skull. His left hand moved uncertainly to his head, which felt sticky, covered with oil, and then his body came back to him in the wake of that movement. He felt sharp, stabbing sensations in his forehead before losing consciousness.

Someone called his name from a great distance, from beyond a horizon which was dark as the pampas at twilight. A woman's voice, but it did not sound like Esme's or Cecilia's or Teresa's. Something cool was pressed to his forehead. The voice sounded closer, and when he opened his eyes there was a woman he did not recognize.

"Carlos? Carlos? Can you hear me?"

He tried to speak but no words came. He nodded and then lay rigid to avoid the pain. With gentle, soft hands Emilia Lagoda and another woman helped him sit up.

"It's Emilia, Emilia Lagoda."

She looked very far away and her voice sounded hollow, a melody played on empty gasoline drums. Then he saw the arm raising the club to the top of its arc, the man's face, contemptuous, full of hatred. Teresa screamed. "No!" he shouted as he tried to get out of bed, but his legs felt empty, as if there were no bones in them. Then the pain left him and the room went white.

The next thing he remembered was Esme sitting by the bed holding his hand. Apparently she had been talking to him for some time, but the first word that made any sense was "concussion." She looked worried and her eyes were red from crying. Behind her nurses came and went in a dizzy world of motion, their double peaked hats like gulls in a high wind, the mothers' scarves stiffened with grief.

"Teresa?" he said. He did not feel his lips move, but Esme smiled, so he must have actually spoken. He saw the club again, heard Teresa crying, and looked at Esme. Peaked hats moved crazily at the foot of the bed.

"She will be all right. Rest."

"It wasn't a dream," he shouted. "Tell me!"

He felt the pressure of her fingers.

"They can't keep her, Carlos. She'll be home soon, like Raimundo."

A nurse with a florid face appeared.

"The doctor wants you to have another," she said, inserting a needle into his left arm. He felt his eyelids flutter.

"It's my fault."

"No," Esme answered, "no one's fault."

He wanted to talk to Esme, to Cecilia, but his vision was clouded with white scarves, and he heard voices in the dark calling names.

In his dream the guitar felt like metal, the notes sounded brittle, the walls of the cave were covered with hoarfrost and ice. When he struck a chord Cecilia appeared, beckoning him further inside. Voices filled the darkness as he followed her toward the flickering yellow light and he heard Guzman's voice rising above the others. The fire at the end of the cave made the ice-wall glisten and dance with its rising and falling flames. Teresa was standing on a stage, or a platform. She did not appear to be distressed, only confused, as she looked at Cecilia, who was rigid and silent while the generals argued over who they belonged to. Then he turned and saw other people trapped behind the ice and thought he heard them calling his name. He understood that he should play and immediately put his right foot on a rock and bent over his guitar, which reflected a face twisted into a blue abstract of his own. There was a melody he must compose. That was what the voices were asking for. He discovered chords that were strange and beautiful, but they could not be resolved into melody and he played them louder as one of the general's grabbed Teresa's arm, another Cecilia's, and led them into the ice wall, pushed them through it. As they did the wall turned solid, a deep cold blue, and he could no longer see the people but he still heard their voices, the names they were calling. He knew the ice would shatter if he found the melody and he tried again and heard only the same harsh, odd chords. Then he was beating on the ice with the guitar, the lovely rosewood of the Ramirez Cecilia had given him breaking, and he heard all the voices crying, frightened, alone.

# 17.

He returned to the dream whenever he slept, fearing it so much that he fought the drugs that took him there like a frantic swimmer caught in an undertow. When he woke, sweating and wild-eyed, Esme or Emilia or I tried to calm him. For a long time he could hardly speak and there was a terrible disjunction between what he remembered of the dream and his words, which tumbled out like dice from a cup. That was the worst of it for me. I was afraid the thugs had been more successful than they hoped, that they might have taken his gift as well as his daughter.

Fortunately the dream vanished by the end of the week and with it the problem with his speech. He said that the pain and dizziness had subsided, but when the relative calm descended on him Carlos almost wished for the other because now he could think clearly about what had happened.

Esme and Emilia came in the morning, I arrived in the afternoon, and the nurses looked in regularly, their starched hats still mementos of scarves or gulls. The light coming through the venetian blinds cast rigid patterns on the white sheets. One day he stared at the pattern for a long time and began to weep. He said he knew what was going to happen to Teresa and the sound of his voice as he spoke was hateful to him.

The room would be close enough to the one where they kept Cecilia so that she could see the guards taking Teresa in and out, could see the terrified expression on her daughter's face. The guards would want her to hear the screams when they applied the belts, or hoses, or wires. Carlos closed his eyes in an attempt to shut out what they were going to do, but it did no good. It was as if he were with Cecilia and they were being forced to listen as Teresa screamed "No! No!" as first one and then another of the guards forced himself between her legs.

One afternoon, when we'd all gone home, Carlos threw the sheets aside, sat up, and felt a searing pain burning through his head. He fell back onto the pillow but then he was up again and slipping on his bloody clothes. He heard a nurse call his name just as he rounded the corridor and ran for the elevator. An old man held a bouquet close to his chest as he stared at Carlos in his bloody clothes. "It's all right," Carlos said, but the man only nodded and left as fast as his spindly legs could carry him.

The concussion made everything elongated, as in a Lautrec poster. Carlos walked slowly, his sore, battered body supporting his head as if it were a basketful of eggs. Buildings receded toward the heart of the city, swerved left and right, while the traffic melted into long lines of headlights and shiny windows. He stopped whenever the dizziness was too strong and people responded as if he were a drunk who'd lost his way after a violent night of wine and milongas and unfocused hate.

When the dizziness went away he proceeded slowly, as confused as if he were from the provinces, or another country. Before the club had hung suspended over him, the signet ring of the hand holding it gleaming in the light, before Teresa's shouts, Buenos Aires could always comfort him, presenting itself as a house one had lived in for many years. He remembered that on the way home after the premiere of *The Names* the city had never been more beautiful, but the generals had taken it away. As he walked along Chapala he sensed that even the air had lost its crispness and everywhere he looked things saddened him. Spanish balconies jutted over the street like heavy parodies of themselves. Buildings he'd once loved for their elegance seemed excrescences of clotted stone and concrete, the windows he passed everywhere reflecting nothing but ugliness and despair.

The cab driver hesitated when he stopped and saw the condition Carlos was in. He reached back and opened the door only after Carlos rummaged through his pockets and held out a handful of notes.

It was the same in the cab as it had been on the sidewalks. Plane trees and poplars no longer glowed with luminescent green. When they passed the plaza where he and Cecilia once spent lazy afternoons he saw only brown splotches of dead grass, withered leaves, bits of paper blown into the air which was thick with dust and diesel fumes. Everything had the look of winter, and he wondered if the seasons had changed while he was in the hospital, if somehow a rind of ice had formed on all living things and, dissipated by a feeble sun, left only dead hopes and withered leaves.

From the moment he'd settled himself in the cab he was preparing for what he would see at home, and the pictures called up in his imagination were so terrible that he wondered if it might not be better to simply take a room in a hotel somewhere, to buy some new clothes. But it would do no good to avoid his house. As the cab turned into Calle Cordova he wanted to see the wreckage, believing it would help him overcome any hesitation that might keep him from what he must do.

To his surprise the place looked as it always did when he let himself in the front door. Esme or Emilia had cleaned things up, righted the furniture, straightened the pictures, made the beds. No one could guess what had happened there only days earlier. It was as if a slate had been wiped clean, and as Carlos went from room to room he thought that this kindness of his friends, this consideration, was a greater gift than they could have imagined. His house was now an image of the generals' desire to annihilate, sweep away, and its cleanliness and order were goads to him, as sharp as banderillos piercing the flesh of some hapless bull on a Sunday afternoon. With this image of their desire, this neat, ordered house that appeared to have no history of violence fixed deeply in his mind, Carlos went into the bathroom and saw a face in the mirror that was almost a stranger's. The eyes were underscored with dark circles and the face out of which they glared was distorted by rage. As he shaved Carlos welcomed the fierceness of that strange face, studied it gratefully, even reverently, for he knew it was necessary to look like that, that the memory of this face later in the day would help him act before he could become reasonable again, civilized.

On the way through the living room he glanced at Cecilia's pictures, Teresa's, and then slammed the door. In the garage he unlocked a cabinet, took out his father's old Mannlicher, loaded it, and put it on the floor of the passenger side of the Peugeot.

As Carlos drove away from Calle Cordova he chastized himself for being so naïve, so stupid. He realized that all along he had held to a belief in the generals' essential humanity, even when he heard the awful stories from the people in his garden, even when he had to see what happened as he entered those stories and tried to change their direction. Some element of decency, he'd thought, had to be buried in their minds, but as he drove it seemed to him that it had simply been a matter of distance obscuring what he could see very clearly now. Not having witnessed Cecilia's abduction, his sense of the generals was fed more by images conjured for others than by personal experience. But he had been there when they took Teresa, heard the terror in her voice, saw the face of the man with the signet ring, which was the same impassive face of General Guzman, of all of the generals. Until that very instant the generals' power had seemed huge, a cenotaph ten times the size of the one in the Plaza de Mayo, but despite the shadow it cast on Argentina he had felt outside its darkness. Now, as he entered the traffic of the inner city, he understood that he had never been outside it. Everyone in the city was inside the shadow, the ice cave, and they were all looking at the face of something with no reason, something insane. The tilt and curve of buildings echoed his dream and he knew that in turn he was being dreamed by Guzman and the others, that he had been living inside their imagination, not on the fringes, deeply immersed in something that had only the desire to annihilate. All of them were trapped inside and he was more firm than ever in his resolve to break the ice wall with an act they could not ignore. As he pulled into the parking lot he knew that the yellow light at the end of the cave had come from the Casa Rosada.

Carlos waited for more than an hour until the soldiers started coming down the steps at five, when the cathedral bells began to ring. They came in groups of three or four, confident, smug, ignorant that he was watching. Guzman was talking to an aide and they paused for a moment at the bottom of the stairs before the lieutenant joined a group of junior officers and Guzman proceeded to the parking lot and his blue Mercedes 450. As he eased out of the lot and onto the boulevard Carlos started the Peugeot and pulled into traffic a few cars behind.

When they reached the suburbs and Guzman turned onto the highway Carlos switched on the radio, turned to several stations searching for familiar music, switched off. The popular songs aggravated him. Besides, things were happening to his vision. Light reflected from the bumpers of the cars ahead caused sharp pain in his eyes and made him dizzy. When he concentrated on the road directly ahead he was all right, but if the glare entered his eyes, or he turned his head left or right, he felt vertiginous, almost sick. He relaxed his grip on the steering wheel, cautioned himself to remain cool, calm.

Ahead the Mercedes pulled into the right-hand lane and Carlos followed it down the off-ramp. Minutes later he watched the general turn left into a residential street lined by large houses set far back from the road. The Mercedes pulled into a driveway and its taillights gleamed brightly before Guzman took his foot off the brake.

Carlos parked on the other side of the street a few houses away. It was dark enough so that no one would be able to see the rifle, but at that point he did not care. There was no way to stop him. He was going to make a different kind of story, one the generals would understand.

Just as Guzman got out, the front door of his house opened and a girl of about fifteen appeared and started across the lawn toward her father, who was framed in the sights of Carlos' Mannlicher. Guzman blurred, the gun seemed to waver an instant in Carlos' hands, then Guzman was in focus again and Carlos had to look up from the sight. Without the magnification Guzman was any father tired at the end of the day and happy to listen to what his daughter had to say. Carlos felt disgusted, appalled by his sentimentality. He bent to the sight again just as the girl approached her father, whose skull was now centered in the crosshairs. Guzman could not have been a better target, but Carlos knew he would not stand still for long, that in an instant he was going to move toward the girl. And at that critical moment Carlos could do no more than look.

The Mannlicher's sight was very sensitive, the finely machined steel cylinder gave him Guzman on a silver platter, and he could do no more than look. The girl appeared in the sight, the left side of her face, as she reached up and kissed her father on the cheek. The trigger felt warm, his hand felt like an extension of the gun, and his will wanted him to squeeze, even at the cost of splattering the girl with her father's brains. It would be just. There were a hundred people in the city, a thousand, who would say she deserved it because she was Guzman's daughter. Carlos continued to look, remembered that at the Casa Rosada the light had gleamed on Guzman's medals, on the braid circling his left shoulder, that the light had seemed the very pith and essence of evil. Yet here he was, outlined in the Mannlicher's expensive sight, listening to his daughter chatter about something that happened to her at school, asking a favor, cajoling him in the way daughters have with fathers. When Guzman began moving toward the house Carlos tracked him in the sight all the way across the lawn. It was still not too late, not even when Guzman reached for the door, opened it, and the girl grabbed his hat. Then they disappeared inside.

Carlos' hands trembled when he put the gun on the floor. He gripped the steering wheel so hard that he could see his knuckles growing white even in the twilight, the tendons rigid against the backs of his hands. "Teresa!" he said, "Cecilia!" He saw them going through countless daily rituals, gathered around the table for dinner, Teresa listened hopefully to his stories in the garden. And then he felt ashamed, as if he had betrayed some deep mystery that was sanctified by his feeling for his wife and daughter. He wanted to ask their forgiveness for his weakness, to explain that he had to go as far as he did to know it would have done no good to feel the weapon jump in his hands and hear the girl's shrieks as her father's head exploded in front of her. He thought that and a good deal more as it grew dark. He did not know what time it was, did not care. He did not move because he had no idea where he would go. He remained there, his head against the back of the seat, until it was very late.

# 18.

For weeks after his aborted attempt on Guzman's life Carlos dreamed of the ice cave in which Teresa's scream seemed to echo Cecilia's as it must have sounded the day she was taken. When he woke their voices rang throughout the house, and every time he looked at their pictures Guzman's face was there too, framed by the entrance to the Casa Rosada.

One night, suddenly convinced that Cecilia and Teresa were somewhere near the Riachuelo, he went out and explored dark alleyways, peered into the windows of empty buildings, aware that he was repeating the earlier search which had ended with the snarling Doberman. For a moment he was convinced they were upstairs in a building not far away, but just as the place began to form in his imagination an ambulance went by and its receding siren stole the images.

To console himself he went into a nearby café for a drink. There were only a few people at the bar. Three couples sat at a table near the stage where a tango band played amateurishly. Only the man with the concertina had a genuine feeling for the music.

Later that night, after the band packed up their instruments, a country boy with a guitar settled himself at the edge of the stage and played a series of milongas. When he finished Carlos asked if he could borrow the guitar, and for half an hour he immersed himself in the rhythms of the music. As he played, the old songs evocative of blood and death, of style and tragedy, gave him courage, and made the real Argentina, the one outside the cave, his again.

By the next weekend he was well enough to return to the Children's Theater, to recite the prologue and play the theme of *The Names*, but now the music was different. The first time I'd heard it the piece was purely in the tradition of Villa-Lobos, elegant and coolly lyrical. Carlos retained the melody, but all around it he wove the pain of the milongas, the guttiness of the tango. Listening left no doubt that he'd survived what they'd done, passing through the still-fresh pain of Teresa's abduction to the source of his strength.

Afterward, over coffee, he wanted to talk about Guzman. More than anything else the paralysis that overcame him when the general was in his sights reminded him of the last time he'd gone boar hunting, ten or twelve years ago. He had been separated from his companions in a hilly region soon after picking up the boar's tracks, which he followed into rough country where he concealed himself behind a stand of thornbushes. Suddenly there was a movement, and as soon as he raised the gun the boar was perfectly centered in his sights, just as Guzman had been. Then something strange happened. He said that he imagined his eye and the boar's meeting in the steel chamber, two eyes feeding images into brains totally alien to each other, the boar's instinctual, incapable of mercy or compassion, and because of that knowledge Carlos chose not to kill.

"If Guzman had turned away from his daughter and looked into the Mannlicher's sight his understanding would have stopped at the lens, just like the animal's. It would have been beyond his nature to understand why I was there. Everything he sees is small, distorted by his preconceptions, which are the equivalent of the boar's instincts. To see inside Guzman's mind at that moment would have revealed nothing but dust and mirages, the shape of an idea like that given a cone of wind in the pampas by the dust it sucks from the ground. He could never comprehend that my stories are more dangerous to him than the Mannlicher, my words more explosive than bombs planted in the Casa Rosada. That was what stopped me, why I let him live, for the bullet would have sent me into exile and silence. If, in return, he chooses to cut out my tongue I can write. If he smashes my hands, I can draw pictures in the dust with a stick held between my teeth. His life is a puny exchange for such power."

# 19.

Since Teresa's disappearance Esme had taken over lighting the lanterns in Carlos' garden. On the Thursday following our talk about Guzman, Carlos waited for a long time before appearing. He'd felt ill that day, and hadn't gone to the theater, but at twilight, as an orange glow suffused the eastern sky, Carlos came through the doors to find the garden overflowing. There were more people than ever before, upward of a hundred, I believe, about evenly divided between familiar faces and newcomers with hope and despair in their eyes.

"Speak," Carlos said. "Tell me what they have done."

A man of his own age in an expensive tailored suit said that his colleague, a psychiatrist, had been taken from his clinic. A girl Teresa's age, her voice trembling, pleaded with Carlos to find her sister. Others spoke, and when he had heard them all Carlos was turning back to the young girl when I heard Esme's voice.

"I have an old and dear friend, an artist at the Children's Theater, Silvio Ayala. They came for him last night. His neighbors heard shouts and the sound of breaking glass, but they were too afraid to interfere. This morning they found the door of his apartment open. Everything was a shambles. I was at the theater when I

138

found out, and no sooner had I hung up than two deputies from the Council arrived. It is like they killed all of us, Carlos. They handed me a form filled with legal jargon. The last sentence said that in the interests of public morals the Children's Theater was closed until further notice."

As Esme spoke the north wind made the flames of the candles waver. It was clear that Carlos barely heard what she said about the theater. Later he said that he was amazed Esme could speak without breaking down. She had known Silvio since they were children, had been his lover once, and held him in high regard despite his cynicism, which she characterized as a boy's whistling in the dark. Carlos saw Silvio bent over the costume plans for *The Names*, saw the neatly manicured lawn of the Naval Mechanics School, the clean, fresh paint, the sterile rooms in the basement.

"Silvio never believed it would happen to him. All his adult life he had been apolitical, a bystander watching contemptuously as governments came and went. He had been wary since the time I began walking with the mothers, and my idea for *The Names* made him fearful for the theater, yet he felt immune because he had no political ideas, no roots on any side. That was why, when the door burst open in the middle of the night, Silvio was convinced they had made a mistake. There are some very political people in his apartment building. He was going to tell the men they had transposed numbers, gotten the wrong floor, but when he went into the living room and saw them he knew that nothing he said would make any difference, and he also knew there had been no mistake. One of the men smoked a cigar and his signet ring reflected the lamp light as another ordered Silvio to get dressed. When he began to argue the man with the ring hit him and then Silvio forgot the pain in his face because the man embraced him, as if to keep Silvio from falling. Then pain exploded in little white pinwheels as the man brought his knee up into Silvio's groin. He crumpled to the floor and wanted to pass out, but he could not. The men dragged him out to the Falcon while his hands ever so lightly cupped his smashed testicles. His gorge rose and he vomited in the street. The pain could only be compared to having his testicles squeezed in a white-hot vise. He wanted to weep, but crying only intensified the

139

pain, and so all the way across the city he breathed short, rapid breaths and tried to keep from being sick on himself.

"Before they arrived at the Naval Mechanics School one of the men blindfolded Silvio. It had no practical purpose since Silvio's chances of ever telling where he had been were nil. They blindfolded him as part of the terror. Think of it. It would be bad enough to be kidnapped, in pain, but all that was happening was infinitely worse when Silvio could not see where he was going. Even when our eyes focus on the electric shock apparatus, the scalpels, we at least know what is going to happen, can partly set ourselves for the shock, the squeeze, the first probing with the scalpel under the fingernails. But when you cannot see you imagine terrors, feel cut off from the whole world. That is why people condemned to death by firing squad refuse the blindfold, preferring to see where the bullets are coming from.

"Silvio was pushed ahead of the men into the corridors of the basement of the Naval Mechanics School. He didn't know what to expect and his pain was terrible. Only that impinged on his mind. The pain in his testicles, the darkness he moved in, made fear blossom like flowers in a garden, and it only became worse when he heard someone moan, and in the distance the unmistakable sound of a woman's scream. It was then that Silvio decided he would tell them anything they wanted to know.

"He expected to be tortured immediately, but instead they pushed him into an evil-smelling cell, removed his blindfold, and slammed the door, leaving him more alone than he had ever been. You must appreciate Silvio's character to know what that meant. He is a man who thrives on people, for whom talk of any kind is delightful. He rarely is alone, and even when he goes to his retreat at Bahía Blanca he simply exchanges one group of friends and acquaintances for another. This morning he was alone with his pain and fear and he knew without even thinking about it that he would do whatever was necessary to survive.

"For over a week Silvio will be kept alone in his stinking cell. Not even the guard who brings his food in a dirty tin plate morning and evening will speak to him, except to say that he is not permitted to speak. The only voices he will hear are those of people screaming. There will be no doubt in his mind that he will become one of the screamers. And he is right. When they take him from his cell without a word and push him to the room, he will know what will happen. He will imagine his own astonished voice making unfamiliar, animal-like sounds. He will try to tell his unseen torturers that he will tell them everything, but the electricity will stop his words.

"Silvio will be taken back to his cell and dumped on the cold cement floor. His eyes will be swollen shut for a day or two, his mind clotted with pain. After a while food will arrive and as the pain diminishes he will understand. They want him to live in fear, to reduce him to nothing more than wild eyes and a pulse that rages whenever he hears footsteps in the corridor. He knows, by means I cannot explain, that his captors are aware that the fear of torture is even better than the real thing in breaking down resistance. He will laugh at that discovery until the scab on his cheek breaks and then he will not laugh any longer. He will sit there, feeling the pain in his cheek, gazing at the hazy light coming from a window high on the wall opposite the door. He will become more and more aware of how narrow the cell is, how his life has been reduced to pain and half-light.

"In normal lives, in countries far from Argentina, a month is no measure of time at all. When you work, pass time with people you love, go to the market, the cleaners, fill your car with gasoline, four weeks slip by impossibly fast, like the image in bad movies of the pages of a calendar blowing away. But when you are in the basement of the Naval Mechanics School, in Puesta Vasco, wherever they keep us, a month is a lifetime. I would have thought that my old friend Silvio could not have endured the pain. I would have thought that the isolation and terror would have broken him, that it would have touched a weakness in his character. And that would be wrong. Things happen in these places that split the real person open, and what will happen to Silvio will be remarkable.

He begins his imprisonment this morning willing to say anything, to disgrace himself, if that is necessary, or implicate innocent people. But by the time Silvio is returned to his cell after his second session with the machine he will understand his captors better. They know that people in pain, unless they seek martyrdom, do exactly what Silvio plans. He will realize they have never been interested in his information, that the pain they give him is both punishment and a gift, for its own sake. He will be punished because he happens to be part of the Children's Theater where *The Names* was produced, where I work, or worked. There will be a moment when Silvio hates me and I understand it, but at that very point he will come to a realization I would never have thought possible, seeing me and Cecilia and Teresa and Esme as people he loves, and through us he will see all of you.

"I cannot save him, Esme. The moment you spoke his name I knew that he was one of those I could do nothing about. Sometime in the next few weeks they will do unspeakable things to him and afterwards he will be trundled unconscious into a helicopter, the machine will rise into the night, and somewhere over the sea they will kick him out the door. He will float far out to sea, but his spirit will be at rest in ways none of us who knew him would have supposed.

"Silvio will know what is going to happen to him, and why they decide to kill him and not the man in the next cell will not matter. He knows it will be chance, the mood of those who give orders. His knowledge will be absolute, and his eyes will give off a light, profound and deep. To the end he will seem to his torturers merely an especially resistant case, a man with no calluses on his hands, with an educated accent, who seems not so much impervious to pain, as beyond it.

A week before he loses his ability to think Silvio will crawl across the floor of his cell where he has seen a tiny piece of wire. All day, with infinite patience, because he will be injured in a way that makes movement of any kind difficult, all day long he will work with that piece of metal on the concrete wall. When it grows too dark to see he will work by feel. What he will inscribe on the wall is this: I AM SILVIO AYALA, AN ARGENTINE. WE ARE LEGION. When they take him later and destroy his body they will think that he was finally insensate. The day they kill him Silvio will be slumped, barely conscious, in a chair. He will not be able to raise his chin more than half an inch from his chest. He will cough blood. His guards will think they are hearing a death rattle, and one will make a joke about it. That is when they will hear Silvio, when one of them bends until his ear just about touches Silvio's mouth. 'I am Silvio Ayala,' he will say. 'An Argentine. We are legion.' The guard will hit him then and send him sprawling on the floor.

"I wish that I could save Silvio from the sea, where his body will float, moved by the slightest ripple, a flower of death on the blue sea still within sight of the shore. I cannot, but I can tell you that Silvio will refuse them everything but his death. His courage remains alive and it will defeat them in the end."

Carlos stayed in the garden with Esme for a while after the people left. They didn't speak, but simply sat side by side, holding hands. His throat was dry, his heart empty, his head an echo chamber of thoughts, fleeting glances of Silvio, Cecilia, Teresa. He saw Silvio sinking into the sea and followed him down and down until Carlos was in the cave again, surrounded by ice-rimmed walls. He heard children calling the names and then Cecilia was speaking, but he could not make out what she said over the roaring water.

"What?" he said, "what is it?"

# 20.

Carlos spent the next few days comforting Esme. When she decided to leave the city and visit her family in the interior he was saddened but relieved. It felt as if his whole life had been devoted to tending the misery of friends and strangers, so that he hadn't been able to grieve for Teresa. After Esme left he had a bad time of it. Teresa filled his heart, and whenever he thought of her he thought of Cecilia, of Silvio, and finally, because he could not avoid it, of his other loss, the theater.

The next time I saw him after the terrible story about Silvio Ayala was at the Raphael. When he came in I asked if he wanted a drink but he shook his head.

"I want company, Martín. Finish your beer and come with me to the theater."

As he pulled into the parking lot the place where Silvio used to leave his Triumph looked barren as the pampas and Carlos had to turn away from it as soon as he got out. I followed him around to the front. The last time he'd seen the marquee it had advertised THE NAMES in large red plastic letters around which fanciful birds had flown. Now the sideboards were blank. We went to the curb and found that the main sign was empty except for a few letters hanging at an angle and ready to topple to the sidewalk. The displays on either side of the box office had been smashed and all that remained of the posters designed by Silvio and Esme were a few torn triangular edges. That was bad enough, but when he saw what they'd done to the doors he almost wept. "How could they do that, Martín?"

When the Children's Theater had been refurbished ten years ago Carlos and Silvio looked high and low for a woodworker capable of carving Silvio's designs into the doors. They finally found an old man in the southern part of the city who was willing to do the job. It had taken him more than two years to carve the two doors into representations of characters from *The Wizard of Oz, Alice in Wonderland,* and Argentine fairy tales, and now there was nothing left of them. Rough sections of cheap plywood with the maker's name stamped all over them in black letters had been nailed across the doors. We both knew what the nails had done to the carvings. I knew from the way Carlos stood there and looked at the gouges in those fanciful characters that he felt as if they had been made in his own flesh.

For some reason the stage door in back hadn't been boarded and Carlos let us in with his key. The power was off, so he went out for a flashlight he kept in the Peugeot and we entered the alcove where the offices were. He rummaged through the filing cabinet for two lamps he kept against power outages. After he found them he played the flashlight across his desk, which was littered from what appeared to have been a hasty search. On the floor in front of the desk lay the torn script of *The Names.* Carlos gathered the pieces together and put them in a manila envelope before he went out to the stage.

In the beam of light the children's marks on the worn surface looked like a school of phosphorescent starfish at the bottom of the sea. Carlos moved the light to stage left where, just out of the view of the house, we saw the table he and Esme and Silvio had used. Then he played the light over the chair and music stand at the edge of the stage and back to the sets, which looked flat and lifeless in the little cone of light. It did not seem healthy for him to indulge himself in this way and I said as much. "That's not why I wanted to come," he answered. "Hold on to this." He left me with the flashlight, turned on one of the lamps, and went backstage for a minute, returning with his guitar. He put the two lamps on the table and they made the seats visible to the third row. Only then did he sit down and take the Ramirez out of its case.

The guitar was badly out of tune and he carefully brought each string up to pitch. He played a chord, another, filling the stage with sound, and before I knew it he was into the melody of *The Names*. The music on that ghostly stage had a quality unlike anything I have ever heard. It seemed unbearably sad until Carlos picked up the tempo so that what sounded at first like memory, sentimental longing, became an assertion, and I had the crazy idea that Carlos wanted to leave the air of the closed theater imprinted with that memory. When he finished he sat very still as the overtones died away.

"That was for Cecilia and Teresa and Silvio, for everyone. A song for Guzman to let him know that we forget none of the names. Not a single one."

# 21.

After the episode at the theater Carlos went into seclusion. It was not, he said later, because of depression, but to consolidate his strength. The generals were like a wrecking crew slowly dismantling his life, removing its most precious elements in Cecilia, Teresa, Silvio, and then the theater, with the idea that once only the basic structure of the man remained they could come in with a crane and in one long arched swing of the huge steel ball destroy him. Well, they temporarily drove him into his house, but every Thursday he came out to march with the mothers of the Plaza de Mayo, and in the evening to tell stories to larger and larger numbers of people.

The next time I saw him, I suppose no more than a month had passed, he was as strong as a man could be who had to live with the disappearance of his wife and daughter, the murder of an old and dear friend. Much of the time he'd spent alone had been given over to considering what he might do to make a living, and after a few false starts he had found a new life for himself in La Boca.

I have always maintained that Carlos Rueda is first and foremost a storyteller, whose gift allowed him to make many children in Buenos Aires happy, and only when the generals began their indiscriminate killing did he discover another dimension to his art, which will forever remain a mystery. But before he discovered words as his medium he had music. As a young man he had made his way for several years with his guitar, and it was to his instrument that he returned when the generals took away his livelihood.

We *porteños* love ourselves as fiercely as Parisians, Berliners, or New Yorkers, and our chauvinism is nowhere better expressed than in our addiction to the music we feel is ours alone, the milongas of the pampas, the tangos of the old bordellos. Years ago this was the music of the people. Now it is listened to and admired at all levels of society, although it may be understood only by those whose lives are compatible with the stories this music tells, even those pieces without lyrics. I say this because once Carlos decided that he would make his way with music he had wide, really unlimited choices before him. For a musician of his talent it would have been lucrative to entertain at the expensive restaurants on the Avenida Florida where the tables are covered with linen and cut glass and fresh flowers. He knew the owners of some of these places, and admitted to me that at another time it would have been pleasant and easy to wear a tight black suit and help the digestion of our bourgeoisie, to take the smiles and questioning looks of certain women, the gratitude and envy of their escorts. But such places were not for Carlos. When the generals took away the theater he returned to his origins, to the world of La Boca.

Late one afternoon, when the cafés were deserted and someone could play a piece or two for the owners, Carlos took his guitar from the back of the Peugeot and went off down the cobblestone streets in search of work. He felt as if he were walking through his own past and remembered himself as a teenaged boy looking for his first job, braving the good-natured insults of unshaven, bleary-eyed men drinking at sidewalk tables outside pool halls and bars. When they saw his guitar they'd challenged him to play a milonga with true feeling, a tango with the brio of the old music before it was sanitized by people of elevated sensibilities. He remembered being afraid that he would miss the difficult notes when the owner of the Café Boss listened to him behind a thin line of smoke rising from a cigarette which never left his lips. He'd smiled when Carlos finished and said that he could begin that night. Carlos had looked out past the smoky lights and worried about how the patrons would respond, hoping that what he played would please the beautiful woman sitting alone in the corner. When he'd finished the first piece everyone applauded, and an old sailor asked for a favorite song he'd learned when he was a boy on the pampas. Carlos had played more confidently as the night wore on, and always at the back of his mind was the fantasy that the woman would approach him at closing time. All of it returned to him as he went down the street to the waterfront.

At the river's edge lights danced across the water from freighters making their way to the docks, and those lights were echoed by smaller ones on the boats of the river people. When he reached the wharf two large bare bulbs fixed on the roof of a shed shown on a huge mound of melons glowing like black stones. Two men in worn Panamas hacked the melons in pieces and sold them for next to nothing to the people crowding in all around. The piece Carlos bought tasted sweeter than those he remembered from his youth, and as he made his way to the café district his emotions were as concentrated as the sugar in the fruit.

Everywhere he went the owners said they had no need for more musicians, and he had begun to be discouraged when he entered the Café Bidu, where the proprietor, Manuel Carranza, admitted that he could use a guitarist to play during intermissions and asked Carlos to audition. He played some milongas, *"Ausencia,"* *"De sobrepaso,"* *"A flor de llanto,"* as well as a transcription he'd made of a favorite tango, *"La cumparsita."* The people drinking at the bar listened carefully and when he finished Carranza clapped enthusiastically and shook his hand.

Carlos worked at the Bidu six nights a week and he seemed as content as possible with this new life the generals had forced upon him. It offered some relief from the exhaustion of Thursday nights when he plunged into the pain of so many other Argentines. While Cecilia and Teresa were always on his mind, he achieved a kind of serenity during this period, and when I asked what was going on he simply smiled and shook his head.

"I don't know, Martín. The only thing that's clear is that I have to wait. They come in and out of stories, like ghosts. Everyone else, those the people tell me about in the garden, are as whole and steady as you are right now. All I can do is wait."

To tell the truth, it was becoming easier for me to accept his determination. At odd times I found myself saying that it was improbable, after all the time that had passed, for Cecilia to be alive, but not impossible. I could not even think about Teresa.

Not long after this conversation Esme returned from visiting her family and Carlos invited her to spend a day with him in La Boca. They arrived hours before he had to go to work and walked for a while along the waterfront. Defunct traveling cranes rose above the wharves like rusted storks, their ungainly forms dwarfing the fishermen's dories with women's names painted on the prows. Across the water, over the roofs of the warehouses, they could see the dim outline of the cathedral's dome, a bell tower rising above the mist in a place not far from the Casa Rosada.

After they'd gone to the furthest dock they turned and began making their way up a cobblestone street to the center of La Boca. The houses were run-down, but most of them were fronted by dozens of flower pots with plants in bloom. Gardenias filled the air with their pungent scent, bougainvillea trailed over fences, climbed roofs, even some hardy begonias hung from pots suspended under eaves.

"Come on," Esme said, tugging at his arm, "I'm famished."

They dined at an Italian restaurant and afterward, as they were on the way to the Café Bidu, Carlos noticed a small shop where the streetlights reflected on objects in the window. When they crossed over they saw various kinds of silverwork—bracelets, rings, necklaces. Inside, at a table directly behind the window, a man not much younger than Carlos worked on a silver plate. He glanced up as Carlos and Esme entered. There were some business cards on the counter. Carlos took one and Esme told me later that he went ashen as soon as he saw the name, "Avrom Levy, Silversmith."

"Excuse me," Carlos said.

"Yes?"

"Not long ago I met an old man looking for his grandson."

Avrom's eyes widened.

"Does that mean anything to you?"

"You're Rueda?"

"So Solomon found you!"

"Two months ago! Erica!" he called, and a moment later she came out from the back. "This is Carlos Rueda."

Erica stared at Carlos, Esme, then back at Carlos again. She began to cry.

"Come in, come in!" Avrom said, motioning to the back of the shop. "I didn't mean for you to stand."

Carlos could no more move at that moment than if his feet had been nailed to the floor. He was overcome with emotion and it was purely by accident that he remembered he was overdue at the Café Bidu. He glanced at his watch and saw that he was already twenty minutes late.

"I can't. I have to work, but come see me."

"Where?"

"The Bidu. Later tonight."

As they started back down the street Esme told Carlos he couldn't keep her in suspense.

"Who is he?"

Her question seemed to come from far away. Carlos felt as if he were back on the stage the morning Enrico Garcia came running over with the news about his father. He was watching Enrico, and then he seemed to be staring into the eyes of Avrom's grandfather.

"I imagined him," he said finally, and as they hurried along he told her about Solomon Levy.

While he played he could not get Avrom out of his mind. Later he had a few minutes for a beer with Esme.

"Why are you surprised?" she said. "Every week people confirm your stories."

"There's something different about this, but I don't know what it is."

"Well, don't be upset."

"Finish this," he said, handing her the beer. "I've got to go back."

Just before midnight Avrom arrived and took a seat at Esme's table. As soon as he finished the last set Carlos joined them and immediately began asking questions. He wanted Avrom to tell him about his life. He was from Warsaw, the Nazis had come. Everything that Carlos had said to Solomon Levy had happened. He wanted more details, felt greedy for confirmation without knowing why, and he would have pressed Avrom further if Carranza hadn't made it clear that he wanted to close.

They all left together and soon turned up a side street that would take them to Avrom's place. The streetlights cast long shadows along the walls and as they approached the end of the block Carlos saw what appeared to be a giant spider poised on the wall next to a grilled window. When they were closer the spider resolved itself into a woman's shoe, faded by the weather, with a broken heel hanging from a scrap of leather. A single violet grew in it. At that moment Carlos felt as if he had walked into the supernatural, for these were the images of the dream which had followed his fruitless search for Cecilia in La Boca.

"Have you seen this before?" he asked Avrom.

"Of course. The old woman put it up last year."

"Why? Do you know why?"

"She heard a scuffle one night, a woman shouting, men's voices. When she came out the next day she found the shoe. She told me all about it."

Carlos thought his heart would leap out of his chest.

"I want to talk to her."

"But it's late. There aren't any lights on."

"I have to talk to her, Avrom."

By that time Carlos was almost shouting and Avrom knew he had to wake her. He knocked several times before a light came on and the door opened on an old woman Carlos knew he'd seen before. She was frightened until she recognized Avrom.

"Señora Madrigal, I'm sorry, but my friend needs to ask you something."

"That shoe," Carlos said before she had a chance to answer Avrom. "Do you remember what happened that night?"

"I heard noises. A woman's voice, men's voices. There was the sound of running. The woman was crying and it made me afraid. Then I heard a car and I knew what was going on. She screamed, but all I heard was a name. Then she said a man's name."

"Cecilia?"

"Yes, that was it, Cecilia."

"And the man's name?"

"It has been a long time. Over a year. I put the shoe up in case she came back."

"The man's name?"

"Carlos, I remember. 'Carlos,' she said, 'it's Cecilia,' but I don't think that was any of the men she was talking to."

Carlos leaned against the door.

"Does that mean anything to you?" Avrom asked.

"Everything. She's my wife."

# 22.

I have said that from time to time Carlos asserted his belief that Cecilia remained among the living. After the night of revelations in La Boca his voice was no longer edged with hesitation, with the slightly irritated insistence which always seemed to accompany his assertions, as if he were forcing himself to say something he found difficult to believe. She had been there just as he dreamed. Perhaps the revelation freed his imagination still further, perhaps it was simply time for it to happen. Whatever the reason, as he marched with the mothers on the following Thursday he recovered another fragment of Cecilia's story and, grimly, of Teresa's too.

It was one of those hot days when the trade winds come directly from the Equator. As Carlos circled the obelisk the heat centered him more and more upon himself. Some construction work was going on in the street west of the plaza and the grating sounds of skiploaders and dump trucks seemed too loud for him to think, but he discovered a rhythm to the work, the surge and fall of engines and hydraulic motors making the heat pulse and ebb, pulse and ebb, and in that congeries of heat and sound Cecilia appeared.

She was in a dingy room wearing a tattered dress and he sensed Teresa nearby, perhaps in the same building. As the engines surged and he moved in the circles of women while the heat shimmered on the obelisk and on the Casa Rosada a sergeant entered the room and Cecilia's face grew rigid. Three more soldiers followed.

"You choose, señora. Always you choose."

Cecilia shook her head as the sergeant approached the bed where she sat with her legs pulled up, her hands clasped around her knees.

"Cecilia."

She would not look at him.

"Cecilia, you are nothing. Do you understand?"

She had been resting her forehead against her knees, but now she glanced at him.

"So you say. And I have nothing to tell you. I will not choose."

The soldiers laughed and one lit a cigarette.

"Stupid as the others," the sergeant said. Then he took her chin in his hand. She shrugged him off.

"You are to be punished, señora, and choosing is part of your punishment."

Cecilia swallowed and tried to keep back the tears as she stood up and clasped her arms around her as she turned away from the men and faced the wall.

"Cecilia," the sergeant said.

When she turned around she was weeping, not loudly, or out of control, and she tried to wipe the tears away before the sergeant and his men could see.

"Why not me, instead? I'll do whatever you want."

"Because it would not be instructive, because you have less to lose. Either way it will happen. Wouldn't you rather choose who it is?"

"You bastard!" she yelled, swinging her hand into the sergeant's face. He caught her hand and held it, twisting it slowly until she was forced back to the bed.

"Say his name."

She shook her head.

"You are not even an animal."

The sergeant struck her then, a short, swift blow which made her gasp.

"It's all the same to me, Señora Nothing. Duarte!"

The young soldier with dark skin and close-set blue eyes who had been smoking smiled as the sergeant reached into his jacket and took out a key on a small chain.

"Here is your choice," he said to Cecilia as he handed the key to Duarte. "Enjoy yourself. Her freshness will excite you."

Carlos was running. He had thrown down the poster with the pictures of Cecilia and Teresa and he was running across the Plaza de Mayo, dodging the dump truck that had just turned into the street. He ran as fast as he could through the open doors of the Casa Rosada and before he knew what had happened two guards grabbed him by the arms.

"Let me see him!" Carlos shouted before the three of them tumbled to the marble floor. As the guards dragged him toward the door he screamed.

"I demand that you stop! You must stop!"

He was thrown down the stairs and lay at the bottom for several minutes, dazed and in pain, for his mouth had hit the steps. The skiploader straining under the weight of torn-up macadam filled the air and he heard nothing but the machine as his mouth filled with the taste of blood from his split lips.

That night as he waited for the words the grating sound of the skiploader seemed to echo throughout the house. Try as he might to reach that quiet place where the words came to him he could not get the surge and ebb of the engine out of his mind. He told himself over and over that the afternoon's vision was only a hallucination triggered by the heat and sound, but Carlos was no good at self-deception. He was long accustomed to the feeling that accompanied his imaginative experiences, something visceral and in the blood, which stayed with him all day long. It happened, that scene, or it was going to happen, and he did not know how he could enter the garden and confront the people knowing it. He wanted to be alone. He did not want to force himself past the engine's incessant droning, but he had no choice, no more than his wife or daughter did. And so he bore down, forced himself through the remembered sound, making it fainter and fainter until he felt himself floating, detached, capable.

"Forgive me for being late. Now tell me your stories, tell me what they have done."

A young man said his sister had been taken along with her fiancé at his parents' house. An old woman complained that it was not the regime, but her own bad luck that deserved attention. She prayed for Carlos to do something about it. Another woman said she had tried everything. Months ago her husband had been abducted from his office at the university. He had nothing to do with politics, but now she was so afraid that she had sent her children to Uruguay. "His name is Theodor Hirsch and he has never harmed anyone in his life."

As soon as he heard the name Carlos knew that Hirsch would give him his story for the evening. Once, several years ago, he met Hirsch at my apartment. He remembered the man's presence, the tenacity of his mind. It was as if we were all gathered at my table and he was listening once again to that impassioned voice.

"When the men found Hirsch's office on the second floor of the humanities building he was bent over a manuscript, an old man with a bald head and fat stomach. They almost concluded that they had made a mistake. Each had taken many people, and sometimes they admitted it was impossible to identify a communist from appearances alone. With his bald head and unruly beard, his half-glasses hanging on the end of his nose, Hirsch was the least likely of terrorists. Only his gray and narrow eyes gave any hint about what he thought.

"Just as he looked up from the manuscript they pulled him out of his chair. His coffee cup tipped over and sent a brown stain over the pages, which bore corrections in minute handwriting. When Hirsch protested, one of them struck him in the face, knocking his glasses to the floor and then stepping on them. Hirsch heard the sound as they broke.

"But I need them to read! Let me take the others in my desk!"

They laughed at him. All the way to Coti Martinez they laughed at Hirsch.

"So you want to read?" one said, holding his hands together like an open book. He moved his hands close to Hirsch's face and

157

then clapped his ears so hard that for the rest of the way he heard nothing besides the roaring of his own blood.

"At the beginning those people considered most dangerous, like Timerman and my wife, were taken immediately. People like Hirsch were given a little time to mend their ways. He knew he was being watched and had a choice to make. He made it clear to everyone that he was apolitical. His job was to teach literature, and if truth were political, then he would have to accept the consequences. His colleagues begged him to be more circumspect, his wife said she could not bear the fear, and Hirsch answered that he had no choice.

"For thirty years Theodor Hirsch has been one of the great thinkers in Argentina. He has changed the lives of many people, and men and women of considerable stature count him as a friend. He is known here and in other countries for his writings, which argue that literature is always a kind of protest. It is easy to understand why Hirsch had no choice.

"He taught as he always had, but there were students in his classes who believed in the generals, and so it was only a matter of time before they denounced him, before his name was placed on a list. The generals weighed his reputation against the need for silence, concluding that the university was tangential, that intellectuals were unlikely to cause much resentment compared with the disappearance of film stars, lawyers, even journalists. His name was placed on the list finally because rumors surfaced that he had been involved with the leftists and taught sedition. The generals decided that Hirsch might be able to give them names, information. That was why a Ford Falcon was dispatched to the university.

"Hirsch was blindfolded in the car, and as soon as they arrived at Coti Martinez he was led into a small room where the voices were quiet, businesslike, not the vicious demanding ones other people had been forced to hear.

" 'There is no question of resistance, professor. Before long the pain will be so great that you will give us what we require.'

"Hirsch was pushed onto a table where his trousers were removed. He felt two sharp objects applied to his testicles and then extraordinary pain, searing, leaping pain such as he had never known. Within seconds he went into convulsions and someone

158

luckily realized that he had swallowed his tongue or they would have lost him. When he recovered, the same voice, calm as before, inquired whether he was ready to speak. Hirsch could not speak. His brain seemed numb, his tongue a swollen thing filling his mouth, and he thought it would fall out of its own accord when they sat him up. His left hand was strapped to the arm of the chair and the blindfold was removed just in time for him to see the needle inserted under his thumbnail and his scream followed the shadow of the needle. When it was withdrawn they daubed the finger with alcohol. 'To prevent infection,' the man said.

"Stunned, his testicles aching and his hand on fire, Hirsch was led to a cell with a dirty cotton pallet in one corner, a pail in another. There was no window. With the door closed the only illumination came from a tiny bulb in the ceiling, which cast a weak watery light.

"Some days passed before the next session; during that time Hirsch realized that a pattern was emerging: torture, then questions, then isolation in that pale light. It has gone on like this for many months, and the men who torture Hirsch comment about the difficulty he presents. Sometimes they have been able to corroborate a little of what he says when he is out of his mind with pain, but for the most part the information has proven to be useless. What they want most, names of fellow conspirators (they actually use the word), has been the source of great confusion. Oh, Hirsch gives them names, but they are never on the lists. When they ask him about his friends he tells them that he is in league with Dostoevski, Koestler, Camus. That they meet in a place called The Castle. That they are members of a secret group, The Last of the Just. His captors check their lists, but the names Hirsch gives are never there. They increase the pain. Between shocks, burnings, needles, they tell Hirsch he is a fool. He begins to weaken at about the time they receive orders to cease the torture. Certain inquiries from abroad have reached the generals and it would not be good if he were to die, although in their muddled way, they have no intention of allowing him ever to leave.

"What has permitted Hirsch to survive? The most fragile, the strongest thing in the world. After he was dragged to his cell he lived only in pain for many days, and when the pain subsided he lived in its memory, in the wake of pain which remained like a boat's wake upon the water. Finally, when the flesh healed, there was despair, outrage, loneliness, but whenever the men entered his cell Hirsch continued to give the same names. He was vilified for lying, for stupidity, for not giving them what they imagined he possessed. What saved Hirsch was his belief in the names even when the electricity was applied, the needle inserted, the cigarette ground out in his stomach, for he knew that the people behind the names had already experienced, or imagined, what was happening to him. Each had said, in one way or another, that the electricity and needle and cigarette are the most pathetic fragments of incoherent fantasy. Hirsch believed in what the names said about what lay beyond the pain, and that belief kept him alive.

"When they asked Hirsch why he repeated the names they did not believe him. They told him he was a stupid idealist, that books and life are not the same. They did not understand when he said that those names opposed everything they imagined, that they had already pitted force against force, chaos against reason, death against Argentina. Hirsch knew, even when they beat and burned and carved away his flesh, that they could never touch his names.

"At this very moment Hirsch lies in his cell trying to brush a cockroach off his chest as it makes its way on spindly legs to his pocket, where he is keeping a crust of bread against the hunger he always feels in the middle of the night. He cannot see the insect, cannot make out even what kind it is because he has no glasses. Neither he nor his guards know that his children have been sent to a safe place in Uruguay, that his wife will join them tomorrow. They plan to take one of his children and put a knife to its throat and then test Hirsch's belief in the names. They do not know that long before they took him a former student of Hirsch's was infiltrated into their ranks. They do not know that in the interval between discovering that his family is safely out of Argentina, and the terrible death they plan for him out of spite, his student will manage to be on duty one night and when the others are sleeping with their whores he will enter Hirsch's cell with a uniform, shave the old man's beard, and help him toward a door in the back where they will look like drunken comrades.

"When they find out it will be too late. Hirsch will already be with his family in a house deep in the country where they will wait out the death of the regime. Within days of arriving Hirsch will sit down at the table he uses as a desk and write to me. 'My Dear Rueda,' he will say. 'When I arrived at the house in the country and was welcomed into the little community of exiles I was still very weak from my incarceration in Coti Martinez. We escaped in the middle of the night and traveled only at night for three days before a truck came for us. Only after I recovered from my journey did Dorothea tell me about her visit to your garden. At another time in my life I might have doubted the claims she made for you, but what she said about your story corresponds exactly with what happened. I feel as if I am writing to someone in a black robe who has a transparent globe nearby, an array of mysterious objects to consult. Dorothea tells me I am wrong, that you live a middle-class life and conjured me in a garden filled with the scent of cyclamen and roses.

" 'I do not know what to say, señor. I do not believe in magic. Perhaps you have only found another way to deal with what the mind is capable of. I wish to speak to you about these things one day when Argentina is whole again. I remember you as a quiet young man who writes stories for children. If there is some connection between your garden and the theater I would be most pleased to know it.' "

# 23.

Generals in Argentina, like soldiers everywhere, love meetings, and I have tried to imagine a particular gathering they called after too many disturbing reports had come in regarding Carlos. They met to take action which their private fear of Carlos did not allow them to acknowledge, for it is inconceivable that a general, or a ranking member of his staff, would admit to colleagues that he was afraid of a storyteller. I am convinced they made their decision offhandedly, almost casually, making a joke of it. Perhaps, toward the end of the meeting, a list was passed around with a check in red ink beside a name. Perhaps the name was never spoken. That nicety would fit in perfectly with the scene as I envision it, somehow making it more terrible because of the silence. I do not claim to understand the minds of such men, but I know without a doubt they would have been gratified to learn that Carlos saw what they decided to do but was powerless against it.

Ever since the incident in La Boca where his early intimations of Cecilia were confirmed by the old woman Carlos felt closer and closer to his wife and daughter. Sometimes at home, or while walking in a park or beside the river, he found himself looking at a scene from their lives. Often it was no more than the briefest glimpse, a face turned into sunlight, a few words, and sometimes there would be a fragment added to the unfinished stories he'd told about them. He was always tempted to enter those stories but also afraid that a single mistake, even the wrong tone of voice, would leave him empty-handed, bereft, and so for a long time Carlos resisted talking about Cecilia and Teresa in his garden.

One night, just as he was concluding a story about one of the mothers who had been taken outside the Church of the Holy Cross, he saw Teresa so clearly among the people that he half-rose from his chair before realizing that she was in his mind and not out there in the garden. When he finished describing what happened to Hilda Albeniz he sat quite still. I didn't know until later that he was trying to find the courage to pursue his vision of Teresa, but it was obvious that he had gone deep within his imagination and was hardly aware of the rest of us. Finally he looked up and found me. I knew what he was going to ask, and my only question was which of them he would name.

"Martín," he said, "tell us what happened to Teresa."

Did I know what would follow? Certainly not its details, but —it is difficult to pin this down—I was aware that something definitive was about to take place.

"They came in the middle of the night," I said. "Teresa protested, screamed, but a young girl is no match for a group of men. She has been kept in a place near her mother, although it is impossible to know if she is still there."

I'd hardly finished when Carlos began, rushing in as if it were important not to let my question hang too long in the cool night air.

"Like many others Teresa, my daughter, cannot fully believe what has happened to her. Even when her suffering has been most intense, when the pain or rage or fear has reached a place someone her age should never, never know, in part of her mind she keeps the idea that she may be dreaming, that any minute now she will wake to her mother's call, or mine, and she will prepare for another day at school.

"It has been impossible today for her to believe in the dream because it has been a day of movement and of darkness. Without a word of warning Teresa and some other girls her age were taken from the room they had been herded into and placed in a closed van which drove for hours. At first the girls talked. They speculated about where they were going, but as the hours passed they fell silent, each withdrawing into her own hopes and fears.

"When the van stopped and the double doors opened, the world outside was as dark as the interior of the van. Teresa had no idea where she was, but another girl, whose name I cannot find, said they were in the pampas. She could tell from the scent carried on the wind. None of them knew what it meant to be there, and some cried while others tried to be brave. Teresa remembered stories I have told and she was convinced that she and the other girls were in a story and that they were being led by something outside themselves."

Carlos paused and sipped his tea. His voice had taken on a timbre unlike anything I'd heard before, a deeper resonance, as if the words needed to be forced out, as if they did not want to be spoken. His eyes registered apprehension and his whole face seemed trapped between fear and discovery.

"Teresa and the other girls are huddled together behind the van when they hear one of the cars which accompanied them start up. Its headlights cast long fingers into the pampas and then it goes off down the dirt road. When it is gone one of the men switches on a flashlight, another does the same. 'Come,' someone says, 'you will be surprised where we are going.'

"It seems they are on an old trail through the grass. Teresa feels the grass against her bare legs. It is wet from dew and soon the hem of her dress is soaked and the coolness feels pleasant. As she walks she thinks there may be a house out there in the dark where they will be greeted by men who look the way some did in an early story I told. Because of this she is less frightened. She whispers to the girl next to her that everything is going to be fine, that they are on the way out of the terror that has been their lives. Teresa thinks about her mother, wonders if even at this very moment she too is being led somewhere. She thinks about me, and wants to be here with all of us in the garden. The darkness is filled with images of her life before the men came to our house, and it is so dark that she returns to the idea that perhaps she has dreamed all of this, that this is the part of the dream just before she wakes up. It is so dark that even the flashlights are no longer visible. It is pure darkness, blackness, but Teresa doesn't care. She believes she is in one of her father's stories, that this is being made up. The dark contains all colors. Sound, and no sound. The dark gives birth to lanterns, to klieg lights, to a thousand suns. It is too light for me to see her. It is a white night and I can no longer see Teresa. She has disappeared! Teresa!"

I will never forget the way his voice sounded as her name echoed in the absolute silence of the garden. Nor will I forget the way his eyes turned black when he turned to me and said, just above a whisper, "She's gone."

# 24.

The Roca Express made the five-hour run to Mar del Plata on time. The sea remained in sight on the left, its blue expanse echoing the pampas on the right where heat rose in waves and mirages suggested fields of water. All the way down Carlos was aware of the flatness of the earth and he allowed himself to think of nothing else.

Each of the cabs at the station had a placard in the window announcing its destination: Mar del Plata, Villa Gesell, Pinamar, Miramar, Necochea. Carlos shared a ride to Pinamar with a couple who tried to engage him in conversation but their voices were harsh, almost metallic, and he answered their questions briefly, if at all. The man was adorned with gold jewelry, his wife reeked of perfume, and the driver fell all over himself with effusiveness which he obviously hoped to convert into a large tip. Carlos was relieved when the sign for the Hotel La Piña came into view at the base of a pine-covered hill. The road curved up on the seaward side and the water showed deep blue through the trees. As soon as he entered the lobby he saw that every window had a view of the white sand beach. Polished tiles reflected subdued lights in which the staff moved quietly.

The bellboy who carried his bags up to the second floor opened the curtains in the room and Carlos was surprised by how close he was to the sea. The sound of the surf was strong. He pressed a bill into the boy's hand after his things were laid out and asked for a bottle of Cinzano to be sent up. When it arrived he filled a large glass and went out to the balcony where a warm on-shore breeze surrounded him with the scent of salt and pine. He drank quickly, refilled the glass, and returned to the balcony. The Cinzano had already begun to work. Between the first and second drinks he had been afraid because images came and went like the flash of a strobe light, but he concentrated on the movement of the sea, the high, slow rise of gulls, the two swimmers far out who had reached the buoy and turned back, swimming effortlessly, their arms like white wings in the water. He watched until they made shore and then went inside, lay down, and was soon asleep.

The house phone rang at seven o'clock and it seemed as if no time at all had passed before dinner was over and he had con-sumed two brandies. He inquired of the waiter how he might get down to the beach. The path from the dining pavilion went through a dense stand of pines, and although there was still half an hour of sun left the path was already dark where the trees were thick.

As he reached the sand a catamaran was being dragged up by a young couple, its orange and white sail still bright in the fading sun. Other guests had come down and were walking hand in hand, or simply close to each other, not talking. The sand went to a deep beige, the sea cobalt blue, and the air was tangy with salt and seaweed. A seal broke the surface beyond the surf line and then another and another, each disappearing and coming up again twenty yards away.

By the time he reached the point where the lighthouse rose, squat and solid on the rocky promontory, the other people had turned back and Carlos was in possession of the beach. The wind came strongly, and just below the lighthouse he found shelter in a rocky outcropping where he watched the sky go dark, the beach violet, a sail far out burn crimson for a moment before it was absorbed into the pale band of orange light at the horizon. He knew that he should have returned with the others because he did not want to climb the path in the dark, but he was suddenly distracted by a whirring sound and then light burst from the lamp in the tower, a long, perfectly defined line of blazing white light already moving. In the distance where it touched the sea the water glowed like phosphorous. When the beam turned north light fell onto the beach in a moving sheet and Carlos' hands were white in the darkness. As soon as it happened he left the shelter and walked quickly to the pine-strewn path where the scent was strong as medicine. The single lamp lighting the path was high up and he had to pass through the darkness and he did not know if he could do it. In the dark, his defenses gone, Teresa seemed to be approaching. He tried to think but his mind remained blank.

She was gone by the time he reached the pavilion where he took an out-of-the-way table, ordered a nightcap, and watched the sweep of the lighthouse beam until only he and a sleepy waiter remained.

During the weeks that followed his terrible story about Teresa, Carlos developed the habit of living as if he were holding his breath, concentrating on simple, everyday things with the attention a Buddhist summons in his attempt to enter a leaf, a scatter of stones. Day after day he relived Teresa's death, always feeling lost in the whiteness, helpless before it, mute. Esme and the rest of his friends never left him alone, and he seemed to appreciate our presence, even though he was quiet for hours, as if we weren't there. Weeks passed before there was any sign that he would emerge from his grief, turn away from the images his mind ceaselessly projected of the blinding whiteness. We all agreed that the most important thing for Carlos was to avoid thinking, imagining, and we urged him to leave the city for a while in the hope that unfamiliar surroundings might help. I had stayed at La Piña every summer for years, and when I suggested it Carlos quietly accepted the place. "Look at the ocean and don't think," I said. "Give your heart a rest. Everything can wait."

By the end of the first week he felt better. He drank less, went for long walks, swam in the morning and evening. Mar del Plata's water is crystal-clear. Even a quarter of a mile out you can see the bottom where schools of silver-sided fish make their passage from one side of the bay to the other. Carlos liked the clarity and soon he was swimming a mile or more each day.

Later he told me that the swimming, such an innocent and healthy exercise, was what led him away from the careful balance he had established on shore. One afternoon he went out farther than usual, all the way to the imaginary line that connects the tips of the bay. There the water was so deep that he could not see bottom. He turned over to float and regain his wind before returning, and from time to time raised his head to look back at the shore. He saw his pale body and beneath it the black water. He felt as if he were in the ice cave, his body vulnerable to the frozen walls. Voices drifted from the walls, up from the dark, their cadences matching the rhythm his body took from the swells. The generals appeared at the back of the cave, told him that he should stop resisting them, that he should give himself to them and accept what they wanted. As the swells rocked him he felt as if the current no longer pushed toward shore but toward the ocean bottom. The generals pleaded for him to give up his resistance, give up the body kept afloat by the air he breathed. And there was no question that their invitation was appealing. He felt the pull of desire to enter into the dark water as he faced the sun, his eyes full of light. Just then a swell sent a thin film of water over his face, the merest half-inch of water through which he still saw the sun and sky and there was a moment when he was at the verge, the very edge of resistance. He actually saw his descent into the dark, the bubbles rising from depleted lungs, felt the heaviness of limbs. Then a roaring sound brought him back and as he turned over he saw a motorboat with two couples in it speeding toward shore. He followed, and with each stroke his body moved more quickly through the lightening water until he was swimming like someone possessed, as if some cold, sleek thing had brushed against him in the water. When he reached shore his heart was going madly and he ran far up on the beach before collapsing on the hot sand. It was then that he understood how close he had come. I remember waiting for him to complete the thought and I should not have been surprised. If he had given up, he would have killed Cecilia. If he had gone down into the water, she too would have descended. I did not understand and he said he did not expect me to. It was because she was only alive in his imagination.

Carlos stayed on at Pinamar for another week. Teresa was permitted a place in his thoughts, his instincts telling him that she must be allowed to wander in his life, as he wandered on the beach. All week long he tested his will against the water, and at night against the lighthouse beam. All week long everything he saw was filtered through the thin veil of water that had washed over him. He did not leave until he was certain of what he had seen.

# 25.

On the night train back to Buenos Aires Carlos passed through his own ghost. He had gone to Mar del Plata silent and empty, afraid, though he did not say so at the time, that he could no longer endure the pain of telling stories. Three weeks later, having refused the call of the water, the Express rocking from side to side as the darkness flew by beyond the windows, he was aware of a grim, impassioned exchange that was taking place at that very moment—the emptiness left in his heart by Teresa's death was being filled by a profound sense of Cecilia's presence.

On the Thursday following his return Carlos marched in the Plaza de Mayo as usual, carrying his poster with Teresa's and Cecilia's pictures, Teresa's outlined in black. As soon as he'd arrived in the plaza he had known something was wrong. When he asked Dolores Ocampo she told him that everyone was in mourning for Hermione Benveniste.

"A year ago, when they took her oldest son, Hermione sent the two teenagers to a safe place in Patagonia. Last week she learned that they had been taken."

Carlos entered the march beside Hermione, and when it was over he tried to console her.

"Thank you, señor. I am not sure what I will do now. There does not seem to be much hope left."

She looked around the plaza, stared for a long time at the Casa Rosada, her eyes bright with tears.

"But who knows, eh? Perhaps some of my children will reappear."

That evening, before he went home to prepare for the stories, we met for an early dinner at the Raphael where he told me about Hermione and everything that happened on the coast. He seemed obsessed by the moment when the wake of the motorboat washed over him.

"It wasn't like the view out of a plane's window as the earth spins closer and closer, or headlights veering into your lane, or the pistol shaking in a thief's hand. I wasn't afraid, Martín, but relieved. I imagined the flames of my own martyrdom, expected that a roadside shrine would be erected to my memory, a stone cairn with a pampas owl carved into it. Martyrdom fit like a second skin, or a revelation, but as I saw myself sinking I understood that they have counted on my giving up all along. They assumed I would follow Teresa into the whiteness, give up on myself as well as Cecilia, and they were very close to being right. But as I was thinking about letting myself go I understood that Cecilia would drown too, that she lived only because I remained to know she lived. As soon as I began swimming she became clearer than she had been in months, familiar in a way I had known but ceased to feel. From the time I saw the crudités, in my trips to the pampas and the docks, I always believed it was only a matter of time before I found her. Her story was locked up inside me, not the linear sequence of words, but something dense enough to be touched. Her story was like a sailboat tacking miles off-course and I was the lighthouse ready to send out its beam to guide her to safety. I understood then that it had not happened because it was not dark enough, but it is now. I don't know why, but the darkness is the price of Cecilia's life.

"I learned other things as the train carried me through the night, things that became clear after she spoke to me. Yes, I heard her voice. I had been dreaming of the ice cave. It was very dark but the voices behind the wall were clear, the names were audible, and among them I recognized her voice. I said, 'But I can't see you,' and she answered, 'It does not matter so long as you know I'm here. You have to think we are already together, that our lives have closed over the emptiness where they cut out Teresa, that we are bound, flesh on flesh, over this absence they have made.'

"I woke before she finished speaking. If I'd ever entertained the slightest doubt, as you have done, that she is still alive, it vanished when I heard her voice. She has broken their hold, Martín, and in breaking it allowed me to finally understand why I have spent so many nights in that cave.

"Do you remember the time when you and I and Esme and Silvio argued about how the generals see us? I wasn't very clear then in trying to explain their mind to Silvio, and now it's too late for him. I feel as if I have been living parallel to myself, aware of what we are up against but powerless to know exactly how to feel it. That is why I have been plagued by those dreams.

"When I tell the stories I am free of the generals' influence. I can see beyond them. But until Cecilia spoke I was always inside their minds when I tried to find her, or Teresa. What I have called the ice cave was a nightmare within a dream, and the terrible feeling of helplessness came from living within the nightmare. Oh, there were times just as I entered the cave when I was vaguely aware of the dream within the dream, but I could never understand that it was only an illusion, that I was giving the generals the power to dream inside of me. So long as I spoke for people other than Cecilia and Teresa I had faith, but seeing her in the cave paralyzed me, like pictures of the Holocaust. They are both images of nightmares—skeletal people clinging to a shred of life in featureless landscapes, bodies strewn about like leaves in a cyclone, my wife and daughter in the hands of men who could do anything they wanted, men like the Nazis in the photographs who looked like giants, powerful as gods. I thought the cave was real until Cecilia's voice let me understand that the dream within the dream was exactly what they wanted everyone in Argentina to believe. Well, Martín, I have killed the dream of the ice cave as surely as if I had planted explosives and blown it sky high. I can see the people trapped there flying up and up, going off to where they belong just as the children do at the end of *The Names.* "

173

His dinner remained untouched in front of him. He sat absolutely still for a minute and then glanced at his watch and said he would meet me at his house.

I decided to stay for another drink. For once none of my friends were in the Raphael and I was glad. I wanted to be alone for a while and try to understand what Carlos had said. In the face of his belief I would have been a monster to question him, to suggest that it would be better to try to forget Cecilia in light of what happened to his daughter. And that was when the paradox struck me. I had accepted unquestioningly his discovery of Teresa's fate. Why was I reluctant to believe his conviction regarding Cecilia? I thought about it until my brain felt like a dried walnut in its shell, and discovered nothing more useful.

# 26.

I arrived late at Carlos' house. As I went through the gate I heard him talking intently to a woman in the first row of chairs, and then I saw Hermione Benveniste sitting very straight, her hands clasped in her lap. She was one of the most faithful of the mothers of the Plaza de Mayo, having come to every one of the meetings in Calle Cordova, and one of the strongest, too. Months ago Carlos had told the story of her eldest son, Ephraim, who could not be saved. I was afraid he might be saying the same thing about her remaining children and I was soon close enough to hear.

"Think of Geraldo and Luis as they were the last time you saw them. I have a sense of the boys sometime in the future, though I do not know what they will go through until then. You still have children, Hermione. I see them with you in your old age. Take comfort from that."

He got up then and went to the end of the garden where the bougainvillea flowed over the white wall and stayed for ten minutes looking out at the city's lights. When he returned I sensed the characteristic movement among the people who hoped what they said would strike him, that he would take their troubles into his imagination. As soon as he sat down a man said, "Señor Rueda, my brother Tomas . . ." Carlos raised his hand to stop him and it seemed to me that his hand shook slightly, though it could have been the effect of lantern light, or just my eyes.

"You must forgive me, señor. Come again next week and perhaps I can help. The time has come for me to speak about my wife."

He turned to me and asked if I would explain what happened to Cecilia. I gave the facts, which seemed more stark than ever, hoping, as I spoke, that Carlos would not hear that I was remembering Teresa.

"They have moved Cecilia from place to place. I do not know why. At first she was in the city and escaped one night. When they caught her in La Boca she called to me and left a sign of her presence there. Everyone knows what they do to women, and it has all been done to Cecilia. She has survived because she is strong, because they have not decided to kill her yet and because, yes, I will say it, because I will not let her die.

"Cecilia has never known where she was being kept. As time passed, and she understood that she would not be released, she began to take comfort in her ignorance, as if not knowing where she was somehow made her imprisonment seem more temporary than it would have otherwise.

"A few months ago she was taken to a place she believed to be an *estancia* in the pampas. The room where they kept her was solid, its walls carefully plastered, the furniture clearly well made. When my daughter, Teresa, appeared Cecilia was relieved, for she had been in filthy rooms, in warehouses, and the instant she saw Teresa she was overwhelmed with gratitude that at least she was not in such a terrible place. Teresa told her that her room was like Cecilia's, except there was more light because it faced south. Cecilia even allowed herself to hope that the quality of their surroundings might mean that they had been brought up out of the darkness, that they would be cared for and released.

"The day after that was the first time the sergeant forced her to participate in his game. She did not know why she had to choose one of the men who accompanied him into her room, nor why the men laughed among themselves. She learned what the game meant from Teresa, and during every minute they had together before Teresa was taken away she tried to help our daughter cut her body off from her mind, numb herself to the terror that one of them might impregnate her. It happens often to women who have disappeared, who then give birth to those babies we call children of the night. Always during the months they were kept together in the *estancia* she glanced first at Teresa's stomach, willing it to remain flat, before looking in her eyes.

"They were permitted to see each other half a dozen times, my wife and daughter. A guard would enter Cecilia's room and tell her to follow him to the end of the corridor where she was let into Teresa's. This always happened a day or two after the 'game,' and each time Cecilia had to find new strength to repress her own outrage and sorrow so that she could be of some use to Teresa. Everytime they saw each other Teresa wept, became hysterical, held Cecilia so tightly that it was as if she were trying to squeeze herself back inside her mother. But she, too, had to find her own strength. The last time Cecilia saw her Teresa said she had found a way to remove herself when Duarte came into her room. She thought of her school, of me, of her friends. She forced herself to see every minute detail in the markings of macaws and parrots at the bird market. She recalled whole conversations with her girlfriends, and as she spoke Cecilia did not know if she could bear to listen. When Cecilia was returned to her room she tried to understand why they were allowed the visits and finally concluded that they could have only one purpose—to increase her suffering, to further her punishment.

"She did not know Teresa had been taken from the *estancia* for weeks. As the time grew since the last visit she persuaded herself that they had forgotten about her and Teresa, or grown bored, for surely there were other young women in the building. It was not inconceivable that they had received orders to treat them like human beings. It was not inconceivable, even after all that had happened. But such speculations had a clear end and Cecilia always knew when she reached it. To go further would mean to enter into the simple, undeniable facts of the situation and that, she knew, would mean disaster. There were some things she could not allow herself to know, and it was during the time when Cecilia consciously limited her knowledge of her specific situation that she began to write.

"From the first morning after she had been taken from our house Cecilia longed for paper and a pen, the crudest paper, the cheapest ballpoint. She would have been delighted to have pieces of torn sacks, pencils worn down within two inches of their erasers, so long as she could write. She knew better than to ask any of the guards, and for months she grieved for the absence of writing materials only less than she grieved for the others imprisoned with her, for me, and when she knew Teresa had been taken, for our daughter. In Cecilia's mind what she feels and the ability to write about it are not separate, and there has always been an interplay between her writing and her life, almost as if, in writing, she were checking on the progress of her own emotions regarding everything. That was why not being able to write was more of a punishment than her guards would ever know, but it was salutary too, in an unexpected way. Silence was almost as bad as torture to Cecilia, the same as grief, and she finally understood, not long after being moved to the *estancia,* that to survive she must go beyond her grief, must find a way to record her pain and outrage. To testify. That was when she began writing in her head.

"It was hopeless at first. When she knew Teresa was in the *estancia* she could not concentrate on anything other than our daughter. But the fact that the generals had reached into a young girl's life and put her in a place where unspeakable acts were common worked as a goad to her desire. She had memory. Everyone in every prison had already made the pain and rooms and the faces of the men who tortured them part of a memory that spread like a web across Argentina, but memory, Cecilia reasoned, memory is not the journalist's friend, or even the witnesses'. Everyone would remember the same thing and her desire was to record more than what was happening close up, in the rooms that were clean or filthy, with the men drunk on the righteousness of their cause, the sick men who had suddenly come into the fullness of their twisted lives through the accident of being born in Argentina. She wanted one day to present it all with a passion equaling that of the men who imprisoned her. Only that would be sufficient.

"She imagined herself seated at her typewriter, a fresh piece of paper ready to receive her words. She began with the door of our house being flung open just after she had put a plate of crudités on the table and was returning to the kitchen. Her sentences were short and strong, like snapshots, but after three of these sentences, four, half a dozen, she could not remember what the first ones said. It became clear that she would have to learn to write all over again, and she concentrated on each word, trying to impress each word in her memory. She reached the point where she could remember a paragraph at the end of the day, but by the next morning portions of it had disappeared and she found herself starting in the middle, or transposing the opening sentence, which would suddenly come back to her.

"One day she sat on her bed staring at the wall on the other side of the room. She was so discouraged that her depression felt like a physical presence. The walls of her room had been plastered by someone who cared for his work and had left designs in the plaster, a uniform series of swirling patterns from floor to ceiling, from side to side. Cecilia realized that the walls offered the answer to her problem. All along she had been looking at an index. To each of the patterns she could assign paragraphs, starting with the top left-hand side of the wall facing her bed. When that wall was filled there were the others, and after them she was certain she could find ways to make the floor, the windows, even the furniture remember for her. By the time she had begun to realize something was wrong, that she had not been taken to see Teresa for over a month, the walls of her room were filled with invisible writing, her words indexed in the swirling patterns of a mnemonic system which, when written out, would yield hundreds of pages about what she had seen and what it means to live in darkness.

"One day, as she was lying on the bed, she knew Teresa was gone. The fact was lodged in the corner of the far wall, near the baseboard. 'They have taken Teresa away.' Her eyes shifted to the right where the same sentence appeared. 'They have taken Teresa away.'

"When the guard came with her dinner she asked to see Teresa and he acted as if he did not hear her. As he locked the door she looked back to the index on the wall and knew that if she did not try to find a way out she would die.

179

"And so Cecilia turned away from the last sentence on the wall, avoided looking at the corner, and for the next week hardly got out of bed. One thought sustained her. How to escape. The windows were barred from the outside, the guard kept the key to her door in his pocket. She remembered the corridor from the times she had been taken down it to Teresa's room. There was a door at the far end and by the end of the week she knew that door was her only hope.

"She made a careful inventory of her resources, imagined every possible use for her blankets and clothes. She examined the table, the chair, then she removed the blankets and saw the crossed ropes which had pressed into her flesh through the blankets and left square welts. She went through her inventory again, concluding that the only useful object in the room was the rope. For the next few days she tried to find something more certain, something with a better chance of success than the plan that had come to her the moment she saw the rope, but there was nothing. It was the rope or nothing.

"One evening, hours after he had brought her dinner, the guard looked in as usual. It was the last time he would check on her. Ever since she had been put in the room Cecilia had waited for him to open the door, look around, and lock it. Then she knew she would have six or seven hours of rest, of peace, six or seven hours during which there would be no footsteps, no laughter.

"That night Cecilia heard the key in the lock and she went to meet him. She had brushed her hair with her fingers, smoothed her tattered dress. When he opened the door she told him she needed a man. His face was blank for a moment, then moved between interest and suspicion. She took his hand, caressed his cheek, exactly as she had planned to do. He closed the door, but it was clear he still did not believe his good luck until she touched him through his pants. She had prepared any number of things to say, but he was not interested in talking. He simply began to take off his jacket. As Cecilia started to remove her blouse she knew that she had reached the moment where her plan would work, or fail. The guard moved toward her and she backed away a few steps.

" 'No. Turn around. I want you to be surprised.'

" 'But I want to undress you.'

" 'I like it this way. You'll be glad.'

"He turned his back on her and began taking off his shirt. As he dropped his shirt and reached for his belt Cecilia had the length of rope in her hands and looped it over his head even faster than she had imagined. Then she turned under the rope so that they were back to back and she pulled the crossed ends of the rope tight. The guard bucked forward, lifting her off her feet for a moment, but her weight was too much and he toppled backward onto her and the force of his weight almost took her wind. Cecilia pulled as hard on the rope as she could, felt the pain in her hands as the guard struggled, gagged, his head pulled so far back that they were cheek to cheek. She forced her left shoulder behind his neck and there was no sound from him after that, only a terrible increase in his struggle. He reached for her hair, tried to gouge her eyes, but she turned away, maintaining her grip, aware that her strength was on the point of giving out but knowing that it could not. The guard pulled again, less hard, his hands moving aimlessly and then, more quickly than she had hoped for, he went limp. She held on for another minute and when she released her grip on the rope his head hit the floor with a heavy sound.

"In another world Cecilia would have been sickened by what she saw when she rolled away from the man's body. She avoided looking at his face as she removed his shoes and trousers. As she dressed in his clothes she looked at the index wall. She had written it all out there during the last few days, every detail of the struggle of dressing after it was over. Before she opened the door Cecilia studied the wall carefully, running her eyes over every inch, trying to commit it to memory.

"The door at the end of the corridor was unlocked and led directly outside. It was dark except for a field light three hundred meters to the left. As soon as she closed the door she heard men laughing in the distance and then headlights came on and she flattened herself against the wall as the beam cut in front of her when the car moved off.

"As soon as she moved away from the building and her eyes adjusted to the dark she knew she was in the pampas. She crossed an open space behind the *estancia* and walked into a wire fence. As she bent to go through the wires the guard's hat came off and she was inclined to leave it until she realized that she would need something to protect her from the heat. She felt around until she found the hat and then set off across the field. A crescent moon hovered just over the horizon and she guessed that it must be close to midnight, which meant that, at best, she had five hours to put as much distance as she could between herself and the *estancia*. With luck she might cover ten miles, less if her haphazard path kept her in the wheat fields. As she turned away from the fence an owl shrieked no more than a few feet away and she had to stifle a scream. There was a flutter of wings and then silence of a kind she had not heard since she had been taken.

"As the sky began to lighten Cecilia noticed some lights off to the left. She could not tell if they were those of an *estancia*, or one of the tiny hamlets scattered throughout the pampas. She went toward the lights, and within twenty minutes she saw the outline of several dozen buildings and the tall shape of a grain elevator. By that time she was out of the fields and on a narrow road. She could not decide whether to chance approaching one of the houses ahead. It was a frustration she had not prepared for, and because she was exhausted and afraid she found herself weeping. Those were the first houses she had seen in years. She was attracted to them and afraid at the same time, and she was relieved when she saw another refuge—the elaborate wooden structure in front of the elevator. It was made for trucks to pass over and supported by sturdy beams which were wide apart. Those open spaces would offer her a place to hide until she could think about what to do next. The fine soil was cool and deep and as soon as she lay down she was fast asleep.

"For three hours she tossed and turned, trying in her dream to hold onto the rope around the guard's neck. She saw Teresa beneath Duarte, her husband running after the Falcon that had taken her, shouting something she could not understand, and then she sat up. The structure was shaking and it took a moment for her to realize that the sound was not part of her dream but the engine of a large truck which had stopped in front of the place she had crawled into the night before. When the engine sputtered and went silent a man called to someone she could not see that he was ready to unload. The voice responded that he would have to wait half an hour.

"The sun was already warming the wooden structure. The shimmering air of a mirage turned the road into a stream and the driver of the truck was walking away from her waist-deep in water. She was parched. She ached for a drink, and as soon as the driver was gone she inched close to the timbers and saw the canvas water bag hanging over the truck's bumper. There was moisture on the bumper where the canvas bag touched it. As quickly as she could Cecilia left her place, removed the bag, and took it into the shade. The bag was heavy and the water was cool and sweet and tasted slightly of dust. She drank and drank and when she was satisfied she poured water over her head, let it run down inside the guard's shirt, over her breasts. She did not want to replace the bag, but if the driver noticed it missing he might cause trouble. She might be discovered. She went out into the sun, replaced the bag, returned and slept again, this time without dreaming.

"When she woke the truck was gone and she knew the time had come to decide. She had no idea where she was. She could be hours away from Buenos Aires, or on the border of Patagonia. That was not important. The question was simply whether she could risk going to someone on the street, knocking on the door of one of the houses, enter the office of the granary. It was unlikely that the regime had friends among the working people, but it was impossible to know. What appeared to be safety could quickly become a provincial policeman eager to rise in the constabulary. But as she questioned herself she felt stupid. She had no choice. There was no way she could travel during the day. She had no money, she felt weak and ill, and she knew that she could not walk very far, even at night.

"At the end of the platform, directly beneath a sign with the name Souza printed in black letters in a half circle over a simple design of an owl, was the office. Its windows were silted with grain dust glowing like gold in the morning light. Behind the window she saw two men, and as she came up the platform they watched her. When she opened the door they looked alarmed.

" 'I need your help. I'm Cecilia Rueda and I escaped from an *estancia* not far from here last night.'

"The larger of the men looked at her as if he did not believe what she said.

" 'The villa?'

" 'I don't know what it was called, but it's a prison and they kill people there.'

" 'Don't worry, señora.'

"They brought her cold meat and a glass of milk, watched her eat and tried to suppress their excitement. When she finished they took her into another office with a cot which was covered with trade magazines. The older man, Ernesto, pushed them off onto the floor and told her she could rest.

" 'You are the first to get away from that place. They try to keep it quiet, but we all know it is there. At night you see cars going up the road.'

" 'How did you do it?' Ernesto asked.

" 'Tricked a guard. Please. I don't want to talk about it.'

" 'I understand. We will take you home tonight. Rest now.'

"She slept throughout the afternoon and later, in Diego Souza's truck, the brothers told her that some soldiers had come and asked them to keep an eye open for a woman.

" 'We said we'd call if you turned up.'

"Diego drove quietly for a few minutes, his face green from the lights in the dash.

" 'They said a guard was killed. Good for you.'

"At the Souzas' *estancia* María and Beatrice, the brothers' wives took her in hand. Five children of various ages came to see her after she had bathed and dressed in María's clothes.

"That was several weeks ago. As soon as Cecilia regained her strength she told the Souzas she would leave whenever they wanted her to. They said she was safe with them, and then they told her about the cousin who had gone to study agriculture at the university and whose body had turned up in the Plata River only two months ago.

"That night, as they prepared for bed, Cecilia asked Ernesto if she might speak to him for a moment.

" 'Yes?'

" 'Do you think I might send a message to my husband?'

" 'Better to lay low for a while. In a month I have to go to the city. Perhaps I can do something then. I have friends in La Boca.' "

# 27.

Even now I feel the thrill and remorse of Carlos' story. Perhaps it was only my imagination, but as Cecilia's escape unfolded his voice seemed to take on the tone and timbre of hers, and when the Souzas spoke I heard the unmistakable accent of the pampas. The people in the garden heard it too; it was clear from their expressions, the way they held themselves. After all Carlos' successes there was no reason to doubt his power to enter other places, other minds and voices, yet even as I was buoyed up my excitement was tempered by doubt because I was acutely aware just then that Carlos was, after all, a playwright. His domain is the stage, where imagination directs the actors, creates their world, determines how they speak. I wanted to believe that he was merely the site where the stories occurred, a conduit to things unseen, but I couldn't forget that he was also a man of the theater with an ear for the nuances of speech. Whether it was conscious or not, the clarity of those voices could have been the work of an artist as much as the testimony of a witness, and the sound of those voices had been conjured by a man who needed more than anything else in the world to believe in what he imagined.

It wasn't easy to think such things, and for days afterward I tried to understand why now, of all times, I resisted what he said. And when it came to me I could hardly believe it. It was the same thing that had affected him. I could accept, believe, when he talked about people I didn't know, but with Cecilia my old world of fact, my pragmatism, my old habits of hesitation before anything I couldn't touch asserted itself. That was bad enough, but it was made worse by my feeling that I was blocking whatever it was in Carlos that had indeed brought people out of the darkness, that my sudden, unexpected pessimism was standing in the way of the person I wanted to see again as much as Carlos did. I felt like a traitor for drawing up short in the face of Carlos' most powerful story, and I don't know how my reluctance would have been resolved if that was all I had to focus on. Fortunately there was something else which brought unexpected warmth to my old bones.

For months the ranks of the mothers of the Plaza de Mayo had been increasing. Sometimes only one new woman, anguished and uncertain, appeared at the edge of the plaza in her white scarf and watched for a while before taking a deep breath and joining the procession. Sometimes there were half a dozen. As their numbers grew, Carlos said the proliferation was like the mitosis of a single cell which one day would become so large that not even the generals could ignore it any longer. And he was right. The march into the shadow of the Casa Rosada had become as much a part of the city's life as breathing, prayer, making love, hope, and that hope was now tinged with a sense of urgency.

The increased numbers of the rebellious, tenacious women of the Plaza de Mayo were not the only sign of change. The papers, in carefully worded statements, began to hint at a time in the not too distant future when the military would no longer be such a strong presence. There were mild, pusillanimous editorials by the generals' lackies talking about a return to normalcy, and how all Argentines were relieved to see that the communist terrorists were on the run, the leftist labor people out of power, or in prisons. And beyond those signals there were stories as full of horror and joy as those Carlos told, but they were emerging from places other than his garden.

Not long after Carlos imagined Cecilia's escape, Eugenia insisted that we meet for lunch at the Raphael. Over a Chilean wine and fresh mussels she told me about the granddaughter of an old friend who had been taken more than a year ago, only days after she learned she was pregnant. When her time came, and she was delivered of a son with the help of other women in her cell, the guards took the baby—simply walked in after it was cleaned up and left without a word. Isabel Ruíz was despondent, on the verge of suicide. She even tried to slash her wrists, but three months later, in the middle of the night, Isabel was huddled in a corner of the cell when she heard a baby cry and she thought she was imagining it and did not know what to do. The door swung open and a guard, the same one who had taken the baby, placed the child in her arms and then led her along a brightly lighted corridor and outside to a waiting Falcon. An hour later she was dropped off in front of her house, at almost exactly the spot where they had abducted her.

While Eugenia was telling the story, two of my old colleagues, Federico Paz and Manuel Salazar, joined us. When she finished Federico said nothing. He hadn't touched his *café crema* and was intent upon the action in the streets, as if he were looking for something. Salazar ran his free hand through his blazing red hair and snubbed out his cigar.

"What do you think it means?" he asked Eugenia.

"That it will be over soon, until the next time."

There was no humor in her voice, not even irony. When Eugenia knows something her left eye closes halfway, as if to focus her thought and announce to anyone listening that she has come to a decision. I think that I was the only one to understand the significance of her story. In any case, it hit me like a sledgehammer.

"They're going to try to cover it up," I said. "How can you be outraged when Isabel is standing in front of you with a fat, happy baby in her arms?"

Salazar lighted another cigar.

"If you're right, and the others don't turn up soon, we can kiss them good-bye. Every one of them."

He gestured with his fingertips to his lips.

"How long do you think?" he asked.

"Months. Maybe two or three."

188

"And then?"

"Then forget. Go on. Lots of fish in the sea. That sort of thing."

I believed what I said. There was evidence all around to confirm that what once seemed miraculous, Carlos' rescue of hopeless people, was being acted out all over the city on a small scale. Paz and Salazar had heard of similar things, but while I listened I couldn't forget the image I'd just used, the callous, cynical notion of there being other men and women for all of us. I couldn't forget because I saw Cecilia, a tiny, almost imperceptible presence, adrift in the sea, wandering in the pampas.

That image stayed with me over the next few weeks, and it came back in a very painful way as I learned that the effect of the lessening of repression was also felt among the mothers. It was as if the faint but discernible weakening of the generals' grip on Argentina had pulled the rug out from under them, as if they had been pressing for so long against the doors of the Casa Rosada that when the doors opened a crack the women lost their balance and tumbled in disarray and confusion. It was clear that while the barbarism was in full force the mothers had an object toward which they directed their sadness and rage, but now the generals were beginning to disappear themselves. That was what Hermione Benveniste told Carlos and me one day when the march was over. They were slowly vanishing, she said, and when they were gone it would be almost impossible to find them.

"The Falcons are locked and parked in the underground garages. The papers are becoming brave, now that the generals are going into hiding. There is talk of commissions from other countries coming to investigate. Amnesty International. And we all know that the generals will claim that whatever happened was necessary, shouting it over their shoulders as they go underground with their Falcons, leaving only dust and bones behind. And what can we do? Walk as we have always done. The past will catch up with us, with them. We will march and the bodies that turn up, that even now are being taken from unmarked graves, those bodies will join in our march, which will take on the look of a dance of death. While these generals disappear my son Ephraim and all the others who have been killed will die a second time. They will become numbers, statistics, and that is all they will ever be unless we can keep the generals from covering their tracks and disappearing."

There is a scene in an old American movie whose title I have forgotten where a young woman is in a room whose walls begin to move. The room is long, like a corridor, and as she runs down it toward the audience the walls close in faster and faster until the screen goes black. That was how I felt about Cecilia. If she had survived so far, whether through Carlos' intercession, or by some other means, she and all the rest who might testify to what had happened in Argentina were already looking at those walls closing in. She would not be among those the generals chose to release, and that knowledge left me closer to despair than I'd been during the years since her disappearance. Perhaps despair was what I needed, a shock to my system that was at least a pale equivalent to the one that had freed Carlos' imagination one day on the stage of the Children's Theater. All I can say is that after remembering the movie I dreamed of Cecilia gathering vegetables in a large garden. As she pulled the carrots and other legumes she stood up from time to time and wiped the sweat from her forehead with the back of a gloved hand. The sun was high, directly overhead, and before I woke I saw children coming out of the house and surrounding her with dancing and laughter.

# 28.

As the generals began disappearing they gave things back. "Imagine it," Carlos said. "If we could penetrate the Casa Rosada we would see them sitting around a mahogany conference table in a room filled with the scent of Havana cigars, the muted light from windows and brass lamps reflecting on the medals strung across their chests. But that is not who they really are. Those worried but confident men around the table are decoys, papier-mâché figures intended to display confidence. Inside themselves they are running, their uniforms flying off, hats sailing away in the wind, running in their underwear, fat stomachs bouncing, running as fast as they can to a closet where clean uniforms are waiting, pants pressed sharp as a knife blade, perfectly tailored jackets without one spot of blood. While they run pieces of paper stream out behind them like the flowers tossed at weddings that will never happen, like leaflets dropped from a biplane moving at a snail's pace above the city. And when we reach into the air for one of these leaflets, or pick one of them up in the street, the first words to greet us will be It never happened. It is all the imagination of misfits, malcontents, traitors to Argentina who have invented stories to corrode the bronze plaque at Kilómetro Cero.

And then there will be gifts. Only today I learned that the papers have been freed from the censors. There are stories of people returning, and the generals have even taken time to make certain that something comes to me. Here, look. They say that the infractions have been corrected, and the theater can be opened."

As he spoke his voice was filled with foreknowledge, and I swear that he forced his mind ahead of the generals', like a long-distance runner finding a reserve of strength in the last fifty meters of a race as he pulls even with the powerful men who had led him across miles of pampas, through deserted streets, through decaying buildings and across shallow streams. Carlos knew what was happening and what was going to happen as he set himself against the generals' disappearance, and that was why, in a matter of days, he began his long quest to help his people.

"No more sleeping," he said. "Sleep comes later."

I believe that from that moment until it was over he survived on the strength of his own anguish and hope, living off it like hibernating animals draw energy stored in their bodies during kinder seasons.

One Thursday I went with him to the Plaza de Mayo. As we walked he looked straight ahead, like a man in a trance. When I asked what he saw he said it was a place in the pampas, "the villa where Cecilia is hiding." I wanted to tell him about my dream of Cecilia then, and it was on the tip of my tongue when I realized that in saying it I would somehow be moving into the realm of his imagination and I was afraid. As I tried to get a grip on myself and understand my feelings, one of the mothers, Dolores Gardel, rushed so fast across the street separating the plaza from the Casa Rosada that her white kerchief trailed out behind her and the young man she led by the hand seemed on the verge of taking to the air.

"Señor Rueda," she cried between breaths. "Señor, this is Raul! He came home this morning! I had to tell you!"

Raul took Carlos' hand, Dolores kissed him repeatedly on the cheek.

"Thank you, thank you!" the boy said, and he began to cry as the mothers gathered around us.

"It happened just like he said," Dolores exclaimed, "exactly!"

It was a terrible moment for Carlos because he saw through the happiness the mothers felt for Dolores and Raul to the emptiness in themselves which he had not filled.

"I heard the wind blowing through their hearts," he said later, "and through my own as well."

He wanted to leave the plaza then, cancel the meeting in his garden that night and his appearance at the Bidu in order to strike out for the pampas. He wanted to run through the dust and into the *estancia* and hold Cecilia. He wanted to do those things more than anything in the world, but he couldn't. Everyone relied on him now. When he gave up the possibility of going to find her he knew that he would never enter the pampas again.

"She must come to me," he said. "Help me remember, Martín. She must come to me. I know that much."

# 29.

A week later Carlos quit his job at the Café Bidu.

"I regret it," he said, "but the music has only been for me. The children need me at the theater to remind them that there are still things to make them happy."

The day he returned to the Children's Theater he found two men out front removing the plywood panels from the carved doors. The nails shrieked as they were pulled out and he told the men to be careful but there was nothing they could do. The nails had been hammered in at angles, some bent over. As they came out Carlos said they looked like spikes.

The first panel came down and revealed Alice in Wonderland. A nail had gone through her head, leaving a neat round hole such as bullets make. Others had been pounded into the elaborately carved folds of her dress, and in removing them a triangular section of the dress broke off, leaving a tear all the way from her knees to her waist. The legs of the Wizard of Oz, who stood beside her, were also perforated, and there were two holes directly over his heart.

As each panel came down Carlos hoped that at least a few figures would remain intact, but none of the fanciful creations dancing across the doors were uninjured. When the last panel was removed and he surveyed the wreckage he knew that the carvings had been willfully defaced. What had once been an invitation to the pleasures of the theater was not a testimony, a battered memento mori of Argentina. It was so grotesque that he thought of asking the workmen to fill the nail holes with putty, but then he saw what that would look like in his mind's eye—features ravaged as if by smallpox, or a wasting plague. It was better to leave them as they were rather than pretend that Alice retained her innocence, the Wizard his spritely walk. For a while it would be right for the children and their parents who passed through those doors to see the desecration because it would make the revival of the theater even more eloquent. And so Carlos stepped forward. Before passing through the doors he ran his hands over the smooth wood, felt the holes and gouges which spoke to him like the raised dots of braille do to the blind, and from that moment the memory of those torn places was imprinted in his fingertips.

After he and Esme worked out some of the details of opening he drove to La Boca where he pulled up in front of the old woman's house. He didn't know what to do when he saw that the shoe was missing. On the way he felt that there would be something for him, perhaps even a message.

He knocked, and when the old woman appeared he took her gently by the shoulders.

"The shoe. Why did you remove it?"

"The strap broke weeks ago. It has been outside too long. Do you want it?"

"Yes."

Carlos put it in the trunk and as he drove off it seemed to send out a little ray of hope.

There was one more stop he had to make before going home— the *mercado de parajos,* where he bought two parakeets who sang to him all the way back to Calle Cordova.

As he drove he reasoned that there had been no message from Cecilia because it was still too dangerous, but he knew she was in the pampas spending her days in the garden in a bright blue dress one of the Souza women gave her. She was in the pampas waiting until it was safe to come home. At night she wrote from her memory of the index on the wall, and she knew that he was alive and in the city.

Cecilia was in the pampas and she was fine.

# 30.

All over the city you could almost hear the generals shouting "Nothing happened! Nothing happened!" Even the lampposts had voices, the manhole covers, the telephone poles, all shouting "Nothing happened!" to the human rights people converging on the city who, as they came in from the airport, saw crews of workers cleaning the streets.

"They have thought of everything," Carlos said over coffee one afternoon. "Not one drop of blood, or a single skid mark left by a Falcon pulling away from a curb will remain. And yet they are suffering at the same time. What they really want is to sweep up me and everyone who doesn't believe in them along with the bloodstains, leaves, and dog shit. They are sweeping everything away, and they are especially attentive to the voices. It's only a matter of time before there's silence in Buenos Aires, in all of Argentina, before the records are shredded, before the bodies are buried too deep to find."

Against their speed Carlos staked his imagination, and once again I imagined the clash of his words against their knives in the darkness. The meetings in his garden continued into the small hours of the morning, ending not because his imagination failed, or his body rebelled with fatigue, but because his voice gave out. Almost always the last story sounded as if it emerged from a well, or the throat of a man with a terrible case of laryngitis.

He slept against his will, giving in to the inevitable, but rarely more than three or four hours. Then he went off to the theater, or secluded himself in his study to write. I told him he was crazy when he said he was going to hold two meetings a week from now on, the regular one on Thursday, another on Monday.

"The stories have to be told, Martín, even if I can't bring the people back. Time is running out."

He was losing weight by then, and his face always had a haggard expression. If I hadn't known him so well I'd have suspected him of taking drugs to keep going. When I suggested vitamins he laughed.

"The birds sing to me whenever I'm home," he answered. "I think they're cousins to those the Sternbergs keep. And I have other things—mementos, intimations. They are enough to give me strength."

One night, when the stories were all coming out the wrong way, and Carlos saw only bones and dust, I couldn't stand listening any longer. I went into his study to see if I could find anything to read and that was when I saw Cecilia's shoe. It was on the desk next to her pictures, like a talisman. I personally thought it represented nothing but blind chance. The parakeets began singing, and all of a sudden their songs sounded like messages from Babel. As I looked around his study everything seemed pathetic. Carlos had gone to war against the generals with words, birdsongs, with a few pictures and a shoe a half-crazy old woman picked up in the street. I remembered everything he'd said about the moment he'd met her. She could just as well have been responding to his coaching as anything else. How many Carloses are there in Argentina, I asked myself, half a million?

When I got tired of listening to the birds and staring at the shoe I studied the pictures on the walls. Picasso's guitarist looked like a ghost, but it wasn't Carlos he reminded me of, it was Cecilia.

I remembered dreaming of her working in a garden, remembered Carlos' stories about her. I heard his voice faintly through the window and I could tell by its sound that tonight was a night of failure and I was convinced that it was Cecilia's story he was telling.

# 31.

On Monday and Thursday evenings I arrived early enough to see the poor people trudging up from the bus stop to Carlos' house where the garden gate swung open and shut, open and shut, as regular as the slap of a loom's shuttle. When I entered the study Carlos would be in his velvet chair, lost in meditation, listening to milongas on the stereo. There was something a little eerie about being in the house with him then, as if I'd interrupted a priest in the midst of some rite the laity is forbidden to know, or a magician conjuring familiars. Carlos never moved. Not a finger twitched. He sat with his eyes closed while the parakeets sang in time with the music. The shoe which might have belonged to Cecilia rested on his desk like an object in a museum, and above us on the wall the angular, blue-white guitarist cast a pale reflection in the room. After a while Carlos would stir, say it was time, and once again go outside.

Every day, even on weekends, he worked at the theater. He did not say much about the new play he was writing, except that it was giving him trouble. "I want it to be a celebration," he said, "an assertion against the emptiness." It had a carnival motif, but he couldn't get the story right. Images floated around in his head and I knew he was trying to incorporate the stories he told at night into something still too insubstantial to talk about. I think the problem stemmed from the fact that everything was speeding up, that he knew he was working against that moment in the movie when there were only seconds before the walls came together with an explosion and everything went black.

One night in the garden a beautiful woman with streaks of gray in her hair, her face framed by expensive earrings, said to all of us that she had come as a last resort. Her skepticism was like a touch of frost in the air, palpable as Silvio's had been, yet Carlos found her husband, traced him to an apartment in a Lima slum. Half an hour later all of us watched a young man's wife making her way like a somnambulist along a suburban street in the faint light of dawn. As Carlos finished the story the man jumped up and ran to the gate, shouting his thanks over his shoulder.

After he'd gone Carlos asked who else wished to speak and there was silence. He waited, aware that sometimes there were persons whose desperation had not quite overcome their incredulity. When no one spoke I knew what was going to happen, and it hurt so much that I was on the verge of tears. Yes, a crusty old goat like Martín Benn was actually on the verge of weeping because Carlos couldn't let her go. The faces in the garden were filled with questioning expectation.

"I must walk awhile," Carlos said. "Come with me, Martín."

We went all the way down to the intersection where he stood quite still breathing deeply of the cool night air. Then he turned to me and I sensed what he was going to say even before he opened his mouth.

"Tonight is the last night, Martín. I've done all I can."

Neither of us spoke on the way back, but when Carlos took his seat and looked out over the people and began to talk there was a tenderness, a regard which seemed almost like an apology.

"I want you to think about the men out there," he said. "Not the little ones, the guards and security people, the drivers of the Falcons. They will return to shops or factories, to fishing boats or to directing traffic, and gradually learn to live with the absence of power, the emptiness of not being able to inflict pain. No, I want you to think about the generals who will never be troubled by those who have disappeared, who will never be bothered that some of us will look for years in the hope of finding a sign of those we love before understanding that we have seen the person for the last time, that all we have left is a remembered face.

"Look hard out there, in the dark beyond the lanterns, and you will see them covering the entrance to a cave. For months now they have been feverishly at work pushing rocks in front of it and when enough rocks are piled up they will drag in brush from the forests, vines from the jungles, so immune to the meaning of their acts that they will see what they are hiding as a thing of beauty.

"Their goal is to disguise the cave so that it will blend into history and no one who comes searching for it will find a trace of their work. Not a trace. Not a single footprint. But the excitement of their work comes from their knowledge that the cave is only being hidden. While they pile up the rocks and bushes and vines they are devising a system whereby, at the appropriate time, they can find it again, like the treasure hunters in children's stories. You see, they believe their return is inevitable. When they think about it they feel swollen, pregnant with death and they are convinced that the time is not far off when their Argentina will finally be born, a pure, clear place as sparkling as a block of ice. Look. Now they pause in their labors, stare at those of us who have marched with our pictures, and they chant, 'Nothing happened, nothing happened,' until their voices are raw as uncooked meat. But we know what they are doing, though we may never know completely what they have done.

"I do not understand why they took the people you asked me to find. Often it was a case of mistaken identity, or suspicion as thin as gauze. With people like my wife it is easier to understand. Cecilia would not be quiet. As for myself, I could not be quiet in another way, but instead of taking me they chose my daughter and my wife. They have managed to keep Teresa, I have told about it, but Cecilia, Cecilia I must tell you about tonight because she is still alive somewhere in the pampas.

"It is very peculiar, what I know about Cecilia. Portions of her story come while I've been alone, others while we're all together. My proof that she is alive is only a conviction that she was too strong for them to kill, that and messages which have come to me.

I have her shoe, which she lost when she escaped for a little while. I have two parakeets whose song you can hear now, if you listen. Finally I have the faith that what I have been doing can be done, a present from my friends Amos and Sara, who live in a place called Esperanza and who should not believe in anything.

"I have traced Cecilia to the *estancia* of a family in the pampas whose name is not in any telephone directory. I have spent hours in the library pouring over such books and never come upon the name of Souza. But she is with them. I see the village, the road from the village to the *estancia,* but if I went into the pampas I would not find it. In my stories I have brought your people home, or told you how it ended with them. In my own story I cannot see the conclusion. I only know that Cecilia will come to me, that for reasons which are beyond my understanding she must complete the story I have imagined for her. This is not weakness, nor is there something wrong. My ignorance is part of the story I cannot complete. The end of this last story, my story, is silence. Silence and waiting."

It seemed as if there was nothing left in the world when he stopped talking. Usually, after he finished, the garden was quiet, but this was the silence of the end, the silence the generals left in their wake, the silence after the gunshot dies on the air, after the scream is choked off.

I don't know how long it took for everyone to leave. I do know that when only the two of us remained I didn't want to talk to him. Anything I said, whether by way of encouragement or consolation, would have sounded as absurd, as useless, as a pebble knocking about in a tin drum.

Carlos went inside and after a while I heard the occasional calls of an owl roosting in the Lagoda's eucalyptus tree. There were faint songs from Carlos' parakeets, and then the first bars of the theme from *The Names.* It is a sweet, haunting melody heard from a distance, with none of the ominous quality it has in the theater. Then he played some milongas. I turned and through the open doors watched him playing the music of sunrise and sunset, love and violent death, dusty paths through tall grasses, and behind him, over his left shoulder, Picasso's guitarist seemed to be looking down upon him. At that distance all traces of age were erased. It was extraordinary because Carlos and the guitarist in the picture looked as if they were playing a duet, and I will swear to this day that I heard the sound of two guitars.

# 32.

Not long after the human rights people arrived in Buenos Aires the papers confirmed what we already knew, except that the number of disappeareds was greater than anyone thought possible. A board of inquiry was formed, and aided by Amnesty International, it began following the trail to the generals' cave. Survivors emerged from the places they had gone to hide, or recuperate, or forget. Argentina was pure ugliness then, and as the dead were counted and responsibility traced to the Casa Rosada, to the police stations and the military garrisons, atrocity became a familiar word on the lips of the mothers of the Plaza de Mayo, who vowed to continue marching until everyone was accounted for. It was only because of their heroism and tenacity that the vultures who came to feed off the sprawling, still-helpless body of Argentina seemed a little less odious. Two in particular stay in memory.

Not long after Carlos' last story an American evangelist arrived and in due course made his way to my apartment. He'd read about Carlos in a flamboyant American scandal sheet. I don't know how he learned that we were friends, but he approached me with the notion of getting me to act as an intermediary. He was prepared to pay me an honorarium and to offer a large sum of money to Carlos if he agreed to give some talks at his establishment in Los Angeles.

The Reverend Johnston had the most carefully cut head of silver-gray hair I'd ever seen, and that hair, an aging pompadour, was perfectly set off by silver-rimmed glasses. "This Rueda is touched with the power!" he said. "Surely he can use the money."

I was noncommittal until he took the story out of his brief-case, like a lawyer about to present evidence. It was in a clear cellophane binder and he willingly gave it over when I asked to read it.

I wish I hadn't because the story carried Salazar's byline. It was clear that Salazar, with his guile and circumspection, had got-ten some of the mothers to talk, and then found others who had come to Carlos' house. He presented Carlos as a kind of faith-healer who ministered to the simpleminded. There was even an intimation of graft and the suggestion of a cult. When I finished I told the Reverend Johnston to get the hell out of my apartment, pushed him out the door, as a matter of fact, and with such dis-patch he didn't have time to protest.

That afternoon I found Salazar at the Raphael and made a little speech about what a filthy toad he was in front of everyone. Afterward I called his editor. It was with great satisfaction that I returned for dinner that night knowing that Salazar had written his last story in Buenos Aires.

When I told Carlos about it he scarcely listened. There were more pressing things on his mind. The play was going well by then, and he wanted to go to the Carnival in La Boca to refresh his memory. He asked if I'd care to come along, but the noise and crowds would have been too much for me. It's a place for young people at that time of year, and I told him so.

I wish I hadn't. Of all the things I've missed in life, that day in La Boca is one I'll never forgive myself for. Oh, he told me about it, took me through the evening step by step, but not even his words were an adequate substitute for the real thing. I'll say this: if a similar opportunity ever turns up again and I'm not in bed with a temperature of a hundred and seven, or wrapped in a plaster cast, I'll go. It's not often that you see life and fiction take each other by the hand and dance.

# 33.

Carlos drove out to La Boca the following Saturday. All the cafés were packed with people getting as many drinks into themselves as possible. A coffee bar across the intersection from where the parade would start was relatively uncrowded, and he had time for a *café crema* before he heard the music in the distance.

Carlos found a place on the curb, and just as he slipped between some dock workers the drummers leading the procession came into view. Behind them the street was packed with people in outrageous costumes, and as the procession advanced it seemed as if all of La Boca was filled with figures out of dreams.

At the head of the parade a black woman with an enormous body spun a noisemaker shaped like a bird in her right hand while giving the beat to the drummers with her left. Directly behind them a brass band brayed happily out of tune. The crowd cheered, danced on the sidewalk, and soon everyone joined the parade. A woman in a silver G-string and halter grabbed Carlos by the hand and then he was dancing with half a dozen people, trying to follow the complicated steps as he went along in the wake of the music.

The yellow streetlamps in the square were lustrous compared with the red and blue lights outlining the booths, arching over the stages where masters of ceremonies, magicians, and comedia people competed for attention. Loudspeakers squawked with distorted voices which blended with the whirling noisemakers. Bottles were passed around and Carlos drank whatever he was offered. A man in a tuxedo jacket and bathing shorts passed a hashish pipe to Carlos and he took a deep drag. Almost immediately the lights grew brighter, the voices and music clearer and echo-like at the same time. He was pulled along by the people singing songs from the pampas and declined the next bottle, another pipe. He did not want to miss anything. Out of nowhere Avrom Levy appeared, but before Carlos could speak he was pushed forward into a group surrounding three clowns who were tumbling over each other. On the far side were children in costumes and a little boy of eight or nine wearing a puffy suit, a magenta cape, and sorcerer's hat stared at Carlos from beneath eyebrows made up in thick black peaks. This was what he had come for.

The parade snaked into a narrow street, headed for an adjacent square. Cars and a truck lined one side of the street and people were draped all over them, standing on hoods and bumpers. Carlos allowed himself to be moved by the will of the crowd, and he was so caught up in the celebration that he did not look carefully as he passed the truck, though there was something vaguely familiar about it. Just then two men put their arms around him and stopped his progress, as if he were a leaf snagged on something in midstream. As he turned away from them he saw the simple outline of a pampas owl and below it a name: SOUZA. At first he thought he'd misread the sign. He was pushed forward but managed to turn around and see the ZA very clearly before a huge feathered egg with eyes on stalks cut across his view.

The crowd ebbed, flowed forward, and he struggled against it, but the flow did not lessen until he had been forced into the square filled with thousands of noisemakers all whirling at the same time. He began fighting his way back, pushing, shoving, all the while shouting Cecilia's name at the top of his lungs. Someone told him to stop drinking, but the booze and hashish had been burned out of his system. He knew he had not hallucinated the name, or the image of the owl.

It seemed to take hours, the way it feels in a nightmare, to return through the packed street, but he finally reached the truck and jumped up on the running board where the man behind the wheel looked exactly as he'd imagined Ernesto.

"Where is she?" he shouted.

Ernesto was startled and turned to Diego, who'd leaned forward to see what was going on.

"For Christ's sake, where's Cecilia?"

"You are Carlos?"

"Yes!"

He grabbed Ernesto by his shirtfront and the man tried to undo his grip.

"A moment, señor. How do you know?"

"I know! Where?"

But Carlos did not need Ernesto's help. Above the noise of the crowd, above the whirling, he heard a voice. He leaned back from the truck. The sound was coming from the air, from the lights, from somewhere above the huge paper cranes and owls dancing by. He heard it again and looked up at the windows of the building across the street.

"Carlos! It's Cecilia!"

Then, off to the left, in the window nearest the corner, he saw her. His heart almost stopped. For what seemed like hours he looked at her. He was weeping, but he could see her gesture for him to go down to the right of the building. He jumped off the running board and fought the crowd again. It was full of imaginary beings. A door appeared. He pushed through it and the dim light at the top of the stairs brightened as another door opened and he saw her standing there.

# 34.

I will remember Cecilia stepping forth from Carlos' imagination as long as I live. I will remember, too, the sound of her voice on the phone the next day, and how I fell all over myself as I wept and tried to get a grip on reality. But those are not the only memories I grow old clinging to. There is also the joy and sorrow of people rushing into the streets after the generals let go, the mothers of the Plaza de Mayo marching ten abreast up the avenues, their photographs and signs more eloquent than speech. I will remember the blue and white banners and flags, our national colors billowing out on the wind at rallies when Galtieri tried to convince us to forget and offered the debacle of the Malvinas war as a diversion. Those and hundreds of other images are burned into memory, and it is right that they are, for to allow any of them to pass into the comfort of forgetting would be unutterably obscene.

No, none of it is forgotten, and that is the problem, for at times like this one looks for eloquence in the wreckage, for a telling gesture, light reflected off a special object, or a word which sums up the disparate images and feelings and perhaps suggests a meaning, if it does not assert one. I have meditated on all that happened, on the mystery of Carlos Rueda's gift and the shame of

Argentina which made it necessary, and slowly, like a flamingo rising above the pampas, two events separate themselves from all the rest, hold hard and fast as truth.

Four years after Carlos looked up that dimly lighted staircase he and Cecilia and Esme and I entered a cavernous courtroom with a balcony running around the sides and back. We arrived early, and that was lucky because twenty minutes later there wasn't an empty seat in the place. We were three rows from the front. Behind us upward of five hundred people were jammed into hard, narrow seats but the feeling was of great intimacy, rather than the impersonality one would expect.

The walls of the courtroom glowed dully with the dark patina which comes with age, or, that day, from grief and rage. Wherever I looked I recognized faces from the Plaza de Mayo and Carlos' garden—María Deleon, Hermione Benveniste, Hannah Masson, Emilia Lagoda, and many others. As a hush settled over the crowd Carlos touched my shoulder and pointed to a boy, whispering that he was Enrico Garcia and the bespectacled, somber man beside him his father, Raimundo. Then everyone fell silent as the judges and the prosecutor entered and took their places. A few minutes later the generals were led in. Guzman came first, followed by Videla, Anaya, Massera, Agosti, Viola, Lambruschini, Graffigna, Galtieri, and Lami Dozo. They sat side by side on a wooden bench, waiting impassively in their uniforms whose braid shone rich as bronze in sunlight. Even then their arrogance fit like a glove, revealing itself in the way they held themselves, and I couldn't help remembering what Carlos had said about the passion of their belief that last night in his garden.

But what they believed was now beside the point. For seventeen numbing weeks we had listened to the charges and seen the horrible proofs—photographs and bones, an old woman pointing a shaking finger, a teenaged boy making his way to the witness stand on crutches. Everyone who attended the trial understood what had been done, and the wounds we all bore were opened again each time a witness spoke. Yet what had happened to our friends and families could not be fitted into the statistics, for the numbers were impossible to believe, and toward the end the charges began to take on the abstraction of a mathematical formula. But when the prosecutor, Julio Strassera, began his summation his words burned through the numbers and brought it all to life again.

The people listened attentively, quietly, and they might have been civilized people anywhere until I saw their eyes filling with the blood and terror of memory, the handiwork of these graying men in the dock before me. And then I remembered another group listening as inconceivable things were brought to light concerning a balding little man in a glass cage who would not have looked out of place among our generals. Strassera's words, eloquent and damning, echoed what I'd heard in that other courtroom, and it was inevitable that they brought to mind Hannah Arendt's pronouncement on those proceedings. For a while I was lost in the perfect horror of her response, "the banality of evil," lost, really, in the unravelable mystery of Argentina having provided refuge for the man in the glass cage. When I'd sat down after that trial to write an account for my paper I'd fallen mute, for there had been no way to connect the man with what he'd done. It seemed impossible, and it was the same in our courtroom as I gazed stupefied at the men ten feet away who had left absences in our hearts and filled the air with tears.

Only when Strassera proposed the sentences did I manage to free myself from memory. For Videla, Agosti, Viola, Guzman, and Lambruschini, life imprisonment. For Graffigna and Galtieri, fifteen years. For Anaya and Lami Dozo, ten. When he was done Strassera turned to face us.

"There is an expression in our language which I want to use, an expression which speaks to the heart of every Argentine."

You could hear his voice beginning to crack, and he paused to stare at a spot on the floor in front of him. After he'd gotten control of himself he looked at us again and his eyes were bright.

*"Nunca más!"* he said, and those two words, never more, echoed through the courtroom like a eulogy and a warning all at once, vanishing finally in applause and cheers and weeping. Everyone had risen, and there was so much noise that it took a second to realize that Cecilia was yelling with all her strength, *"Nunca más!"*

The police officers had the generals on their feet. Videla glared at the jeering crowd and Guzman shouted "Sons of bitches!" Then something happened to the hatred in his eyes, for as he spoke to us, to Argentina, he found himself looking directly at Carlos, who stood silently by my side. Guzman quickly shifted his eyes away, but it was too late to hide the sickness, the confusion, that that brief encounter cost. Carlos responded by putting his arm around Cecilia, who was weeping uncontrollably into her hands, but then, as if aware that covering her eyes robbed her of a sight she'd earned, she removed her hands. As the generals were led off she said, *"Nunca más,* Videla. *Nunca más,* Guzman,"* and she named each and every one until they'd gone.

That afternoon the three of us went to their apartment on a tree-lined avenue, a place they'd moved to in the hope that Teresa's absence might be more tolerable. Not long after they moved in Cecilia had returned to *La Opinión,* and while her work retained its old mixture of acerbity and wit, her arguments revealed an understanding far beyond what you would expect from a person her age. Over the last few years she had produced editorials even more uncompromising than the one which brought the Falcon to her door, and the spirit of those pieces was in every sentence of the book she worked on, which she called *The Wall.*

For a long time after finding her Carlos did no work on the play that had taken him to La Boca. His imagination was depleted, and he contented himself by collaborating with Esme, and directing the children who flocked to the theater after the generals went into hiding.

The emotion of the courtroom left us drained by the time we returned to the apartment. Carlos silently mixed some drinks and then went into the study he shared with Cecilia and came out with a manuscript. It was the Carnival play.

"I've finished it," he said quietly. Then he picked up his drink and went over to the sofa where he began reading the paper.

I took it outside to the balcony where I settled into a lounge chair. Across the street was a small park frequented by people in the neighborhood. Cecilia had filled the balcony with potted cyclamen and roses and you could look down from it into the park and watch people lounging under the trees while their children played on swings, or splashed in the wading pool. Carlos put up three bird feeders soon after they moved in, and day and night exotic creatures flew in to feed and leisurely preen themselves on the wrought-iron railing. They were all quite tame.

It was difficult to concentrate on the play at first because in the park below two little boys were laughing as their father pushed them on the swings. Besides that, Carlos' birds chattered madly as they swirled in the sunlight like acrobats, but soon the noise faded away. The play was filled with fanciful beings at Carnival, and the characters seemed linked to the boys in the park who were yelling delightedly as their father pushed them higher and higher. Suddenly I realized that it wasn't a comparison but a continuity I felt between those children and the characters in the play, and that that was just what Carlos had placed his faith in all along.

As I read I began to see the boys swinging in the words on the page, rising into the sky with their red jackets trailing out in the wind, and I remembered the first words Carlos spoke to Enrico Garcia about his father, a door opening onto the brittle clash of a knife against Carlos' words, a shoe hanging on a wall with a single flower growing in it. I did not look up from the manuscript, but if I had I would not have been surprised to see a white carnation floating like a benediction in the clear Argentinian sky.